The
Word
Eater

The Word Eater

Mary Amato

Spot illustrations by
Christopher Ryniak

SCHOLASTIC INC.

New York Toronto London Auckland Sydney
Mexico City New Delhi Hong Kong Buenos Aires

ISBN 0-439-34251-1

Text copyright © 2000 by Mary Koepke Amato.
Illustrations copyright © 2000 by Christopher Ryniak. All rights reserved.
Published by Scholastic Inc., 555 Broadway, New York, NY 10012,
by arrangement with Holiday House, Inc. SCHOLASTIC
and associated logos are trademarks and/or registered
trademarks of Scholastic Inc.

12 11 10 9 8 7 6 5   2 3 4 5 6/0

Printed in the U.S.A.   40

First Scholastic printing, September 2001

In memory of
Aunt Mil

Acknowledgments

Thanks to Ivan, Maxwell, Simon, and my entire
family for feeding me encouragement. Thanks to
Rachel, Stephanie, and the Shannon girls for feeding
me constructive comments; to the Heekin Foundation
for feeding me grant money; and to William Reiss
for feeding the manuscript to the wonderful Regina
Griffin. Thanks to Natasha Sajé for feeding me
heteroglossia and biscotti. And, finally,
thanks to Marion "The Librarian" Schwerman
for feeding me all the great children's books
that turned me into a bookworm
as a child.

The
Word
Eater

Monday
1
October

"Worms and slugs and beetley bugs. You don't know what's good for you."
—Roald Dahl
George's Marvelous Medicine

A yellowish cocoon, about the size of a corn kernel, twitched and rolled in the mud. A fat worm sucking up leaf mold felt the cocoon's vibrations through the mud and stopped eating. Quickly, she drummed a message through the ground to the others. *A Birth! A Birth!* Within seconds, 253 worms—the whole Lumbricus Clan—squirmed out of their tunnels and gathered into a circle around the cocoon with their leader, the Great Lumbra.

Finally the jerking stopped, and a baby worm, as small as a grain of rice, poked his head out of the cocoon into the moist October air. He blinked and looked at the worms gathered around him.

Worms are very sensitive creatures, and right away, this little newborn sensed that he was different. He blinked again. He had eyes, for one. The worms around him were eyeless, yet they seemed to be looking right at him.

"Why hasn't he jumped out?" a worm whispered.

"Is something wrong with him?" asked another.

"Could be a Nothing Birth," the Great Lumbra said in a gritty, ominous voice.

The little worm snapped to attention. They were waiting for him to jump out of his cocoon! Eager to make a good impression, he summoned up his strength, squeezed his eyes shut, and jumped. He imagined soaring out, turning a somersault in midair, and landing in the center of the clan's circle. Instead, he slid down the side of the cocoon and plopped headfirst in the mud.

The worms gasped.

The Great Lumbra frowned and shook her fat

head. "The vibration is runtly and weakish! He won't pass the tests."

The sound of the Great Lumbra's voice made the baby worm's skin prickle with dread. He didn't know what she was talking about, but it didn't sound good.

One hundred yards from the ditch where the Lumbricus Clan lived, a girl named Lerner Chanse was sitting on a swing. Her skin was prickling with dread, too, from the sound of another voice: the voice of Reba Silo, the queen of the MPOOE Club.

"The only way you can get into the MPOOE Club is to pass a dare," Reba was telling her. "We thought up a good one for you. Actually, *I* thought it up. I *rule* when it comes to dares."

The two girls were sitting on rusty swings at the bottom of the Cleveland Park Middle School playground. All the other sixth graders were up on the blacktop next to the school pretending to have lunchtime recess while secretly watching the newcomer and the queen.

"Here's what you have to do," Reba continued. "Steal Mr. Droan's grade book, change Bobby Nitz's grade from D to A, and return it to Mr. Droan! Isn't that excellent?"

It didn't sound excellent to Lerner. "I don't get it," she said. "Nobody likes Bobby. Why do you want me to make his grade better?"

"That's the double-whammy part!" Reba said, enjoying herself. "See, if you don't get caught, then eventually Droan will notice the change in the grade book, and he'll think Nitz did it! I mean, who else would? Nitz will get in big trouble. Isn't that excellent?"

Lerner pushed up her glasses. "What happens if I get caught?"

"Don't worry about that. If you get caught, you'll just get suspended or something. The important thing is that even if you're caught, you'll still become a MPOOE because you did the dare." Reba hopped out of her swing, clearing the puddle underneath it, and looked back at Lerner. "It's an honor to get a dare, you know. And if you don't take the dare . . . well, you know what happens to people who aren't MPOOEs."

Lerner knew. Everybody knew. If the Most Powerful Ones On Earth (the MPOOEs) gave you a dare and you did it, then you were in the MPOOE Club. You got to wear a MPOOE wristband, and go to secret meetings, and basically own the school. Reba started the club, and when she decided to let boys in, it gained a kind of authority that no other clique had. If you weren't in the club, then you were a Sorry Loser Under Ground (a SLUG), which meant you were nothing. Lerner didn't really care about being a MPOOE, but she didn't want to be a SLUG for three reasons:

1. She didn't like the sound of the name.
2. The other SLUGs never looked like they had any fun.
3. Bobby Nitz was a SLUG.

Lerner stared at the mud under her swing and wished that everything would disappear: the dare, Reba, the MPOOE Club, Mr. Droan, the whole school—*poof!* On second thought, she said to herself, I wish the entire city of Washington, D.C., would disappear.

"It's now or never," Reba said, gesturing up at Mr. Droan on the blacktop. "Recess is almost over."

Mr. Droan and Ms. Findley were sitting on a bench near the school door. Mr. Droan's canvas tote bag was propped against the bench, his green grade book sticking out like a giant ticket.

Lerner sighed and got off the swing. All around the playground, heads turned in her direction. She felt like a bug under a microscope. "Does everybody on the planet know about the dare?"

"The MPOOEs know, and they're sworn to secrecy."

Lerner inched up the grassy slope toward the teachers' bench. The wet earth squished beneath her old sneakers, moisture leaking up through a crack in one sole. Was she really going through with it?

The dare bothered her. She didn't like Bobby

Nitz—he was mean and smart mouthed and, unfortunately for Lerner, her next-door neighbor. But she didn't think he should get in trouble for something she did. Lerner Chanse had principles. She didn't think she should have to pass a test to make friends, either. So why was she headed toward that green grade book?

The circle of worms around the newborn was perfectly still. The newborn looked nervously from worm to worm to worm to worm. Why wasn't anybody moving? Why wasn't anybody saying anything?

The little worm didn't know it, but the Great Lumbra and her clan were all waiting for him to skinch. It was the first test. If a newborn was strong enough to skinch, then Lumbra would sense the particular vibration made by the skinching worm, and that vibration would become the newborn's name.

Unfortunately, the newborn was too scared to move one little scooch, let alone a whole skinch.

After a few minutes, Lumbra sighed and addressed the crowd. "The newborn is too weakish to skinch. I hereby proclaim a Nothing Birth. We leave him to die."

Leave him to die? That didn't sound good. The little worm picked his head up and began moving all the hairlike bristles on his underbelly back and forth, moving forward.

The others waited to hear if Lumbra would accept the worm's effort. Lumbra pressed her great underbelly to the ground and tried to feel the particular vibration the worm was making. A less than nothing sound . . . *Fip* . . . *Fip* . . . *Fip*.

Turning to her clan, the old worm muttered, "He passes the first test. His name is Fip. If he is strong enough to eat the First Bite of dirt, then we welcome him to the Lumbricus Clan." She drew a ritual circle in the mud and sniffed around, frowning. "Where is the runtly one?"

"I believe you're sitting on him," said Rashom.

Lumbra skinched out of the way. "Hoisters, come!"

Two strong worms wriggled under Fip, hoisting him up according to custom. "May his gizzard churn!" Lumbra chanted.

BAM! Bobby Nitz slammed a basketball against the brick wall of the school and watched Lerner Chanse out of the corner of his eye. He had overheard Reba and Randy plotting the dare in the library, and he was burning mad. BAM! He slammed the ball harder. He was also jealous, although he wouldn't admit it. Chanse was new, and she was already getting a dare. BAM! The MPOOEs would never give him a dare even though he had more guts than anybody in the whole school. BAM! He hated them all.

*   *   *

Lerner inched her way up the playground hill, sure she was going to throw up. She brushed her bangs off her forehead and pushed on her glasses, aware that everybody was staring at her. She had a sudden and horrifying thought: With her short legs and her short blond hair, she looked like a baby boy in an antique photograph. She might as well wear a sailor suit. To make matters worse, her bangs needed a trim, but she refused to have her hair cut by anyone other than Mrs. Wellbloom, her old neighbor, and her mother stubbornly refused to fly her back to Wisconsin just for a trim.

Lerner reached the top of the hill. On the basketball court, Reba's boyfriend, Randy, stopped guarding for a second. Looking at Lerner, he rubbed the MPOOE band around his wrist. She could feel her face redden in the cool air.

DON'T GO THROUGH WITH IT! A voice inside her head screamed. WHO NEEDS TO BE IN THE LOUSY MPOOE CLUB?

Lerner glanced around. Bobby Nitz was off in the corner, slamming a basketball against the school wall.

"The singing potato is *not* on the underwear commercial, it's on the chips commercial," Mr. Droan was saying over the noise. "As in *po-ta-to* chips, get it?"

Lerner passed the bench slowly, tipping Mr. Droan's book bag over with her foot.

"Well, you don't have to be so huffy about it, Markus," replied Ms. Findley.

The bag's contents spilled out. Lerner knelt down, setting her backpack on top of Mr. Droan's grade book, and pretended to tie her shoe. She was just about to stand up, gripping the grade book underneath her own backpack, when . . . BAM!

Bobby's basketball slammed into her. She dropped everything and fell backward.

"Look what you did, Nitz!" Mr. Droan screamed.

Bobby bent down and stuffed Mr. Droan's things back into his tote bag.

The teacher snatched it from him. "Apologize to Ms. Chanse!"

Lerner stood up, rubbing a scraped elbow.

"Sorry, Helmet Head," Bobby said. His smug smile told her that he knew about the dare, that he wasn't sorry at all. A mixture of guilt and anger rocked Lerner. She had expected to be caught by Mr. Droan, not by Bobby.

The bell rang, and everybody headed in. Reba caught up to Lerner. "I saw the whole thing," she said. "Nitz slammed into you on purpose. He must have found out about the dare."

Lerner brightened at Reba's sympathetic tone. Maybe the MPOOEs would forget the whole thing and just let her in the club.

"I'll give you one more chance tomorrow at recess," Reba said. "Same dare."

Lerner's heart sank. "But Bobby knows! He'll just botch it up again."

"That's your problem," the queen said. "Isn't it?"

Bobby Nitz was ecstatic. Not only had he sabotaged the MPOOE plan to get him in trouble, but he had also acquired a prize. A package of thumbtacks had spilled out of Droan's bag, and he had pocketed it without being seen. One hundred gleaming weapons!

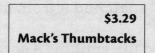

He tore off the paper label, dropping it on the ground as if the world were his personal garbage can. Who would his first victim be? He ran into the school and down the hall to language arts. The room was empty. He put two thumbtacks on Ms. Findley's chair and slid into his own seat.

Bitsy Findley walked in. As usual, she had two pencils sticking out of her head—one behind each ear—like antennae. "Take out a sheet of paper and clear your desks," she announced as the students filed in. "Time for the spelling test."

Bobby Nitz gripped the sides of his desk with barely containable glee. She'd give them the first word and then sit down. She did this every time. He couldn't wait.

"Time for the First Bite!" the Great Lumbra chanted. "Hoisters, lower!"

The hoister worms were slowly lowering Fip into the muddy center of the ritual circle when a piece of paper, carried by the wind, tumbled in. Knocked off balance, the hoisters let Fip drop. He landed right on top of the paper.

It was just an ordinary piece of litter, a label. But in all the naming ceremonies the Great Lumbra had conducted over the years, not one worm was ever set down on a piece of paper to eat its first meal.

No one moved, except Fip. He lifted his head. Something smelled tangy and sharp. He wriggled all the bristles on his belly forward and back until he moved over to the big, black *M* on the paper. *Fip . . . Fip . . . Fip.* Everyone listened in amazement.

Ummy! Um! He said to himself and nibbled the *M* right off the paper.

Lumbra's mouth fell open. She had never heard anything like it. Fip chomped away until he had eaten the inky letters off the label. All that was left was the price. He skinched off the paper, burped, and beamed at the crowd.

Ms. Findley stood at her desk, about to enunciate the first word of the spelling quiz. Suddenly, the papers posted on her bulletin board fluttered to the floor.

The entire class watched the brief paper shower, not knowing what to make of it. Ms. Findley didn't know what to make of it, either. What happened to the thumbtacks? she wondered. Disliking distractions, she quickly scooped the papers off the floor and began the quiz.

Bobby Nitz had precisely two thumbtacks on his mind and couldn't wait for his teacher to sit down on them.

"*Saturate,*" Ms. Findley said. "The first spelling word is *saturate.* I plan to saturate your brains with spelling words." The teacher laughed at her little joke and sat down.

Bobby leaned forward.

Ms. Findley smiled as if she were sitting on heaven's softest cloud and said, "Word number two is—"

"No way!"

"Excuse me, Bobby?" Ms. Findley peered over her list at him.

"What happened to . . . uh . . . I was wondering if your chair is comfortable, Ms. Findley."

"How very odd of you to be concerned," said Ms. Findley. "My chair is perfectly fine. Word number two is *weary*. Ms. Findley is weary of interruptions."

Bobby leaned over to see if he could spot the thumbtacks on the floor. Maybe they had fallen under Findley's desk. What else could have happened? He didn't see them anywhere. Oh well, he had plenty more where they came from. He pulled the thumbtack case out of his pocket and got the second surprise of the day.

Empty. Every last thumbtack had vanished.

Fip sat looking at his clan with a full gizzard and a huge grin.

But instead of gathering around him to welcome him, the other worms were backing away. "A Lumbricus worm that doesn't eat dirt? How can it be?" said Pumama.

"It can't count as a First Bite, can it, Lumbra?" asked Rashom.

The little worm's smile faded. Being a newborn, he didn't understand everything that was happening, but he knew he had done something wrong. Quickly, Fip skinched over to Lumbra and sucked a fleck of dirt into his mouth. See! he tried to say, I'm one of you! But the dirt caught in his throat and he choked. Tears stung his eyes. Through them, he looked up at the leader.

The old worm turned her back to him and began skinching down the mouth of a tunnel. A Nothing Birth. One by one the other members of the Lumbricus Clan followed her down. Fip was left alone.

Tuesday
2
October

"Time for a little something."
—A. A. Milne
Winnie the Worm

Bobby Nitz woke up early, still wondering about yesterday's thumbtack mystery. He tiptoed into his father's den, turned on the computer, tapped into the Internet, and called up the online news. In the search command field, he typed THUMB-TACK. The cursor blinked, the machine hummed,

...ng for any and all appearances of the ...d THUMBTACK in newly filed articles. Three not-off-the-press stories appeared on Bobby's screen. He had to print them quickly before his father woke up. Mr. Robert Nitz, Sr., didn't appreciate Bobby messing around with his computer.

W	— ⧉ X

File Edit View Insert Layout Tools Graphics Table Window Help

SHOULD SHADEL HANG SHOES?

PHOENIX—At Shadel Dance Studio yesterday, a thumbtack holding up a poster disappeared. The poster slipped under Miss Shadel's foot as she was demonstrating her triple pirouette. She landed on her head. Thankfully, she was wearing her hair in a large bun, which provided excellent padding.

A WORD FROM THE SPEECHLESS

ANCHORAGE—Three years ago, a woman lost her power of speech after being caught in an avalanche. Until yesterday, doctors had little hope of her recovery. She was sitting underneath a bulletin board when the mass of white papers thumbtacked to the board fell on her head. "Avalanche!" the woman cried and ran out the door.

TACK THEFT, WHAT'S THE POINT?

WASHINGTON—Check the thumbtack box in your drawer. If it's Mack's brand, it's probably empty. Mack's Thumbtacks vanished from store shelves and bulletin boards. President Archibald Mack has no comment. Located on Bellitas Island, Mack Industries also trains the world's fiercest dogs, Attackaterriers, with his secret "Attacka" method.

Start

The mystery was bigger than Bobby thought. Why, he wondered, did only Mack's Thumbtacks disappear? And why wasn't this Mr. Mack guy commenting? And what did thumbtacks have to do with Attackaterriers?

*   *   *

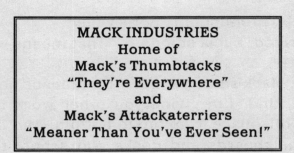

MACK INDUSTRIES
Home of
Mack's Thumbtacks
"They're Everywhere"
and
Mack's Attackaterriers
"Meaner Than You've Ever Seen!"

On Bellitas Island, Lucia closed her eyes and made a wish. This magic that made the thumbtacks disappear, she said, I want more of it. I want the whole Mack Industries to disappear.

Mr. Archibald Mack's voice snapped her out of her daydream.

"Any thumbtacks?" he said.

"Any thumbtacks?" bellowed Boris, his bodyguard.

Lucia jumped and stared at the empty boxes in front of her. She was sitting at the Mack Industries thumbtack packing table with twenty other children. Their orders were to keep making and packing tacks, but no matter how hard they tried, they couldn't do it. The children over at the machine kept pouring the steel, but the thumbtacks would vanish before they could pop open the molds.

Mr. Mack, a handsome man in a sharp white suit, gritted his sharp white teeth. "Stop production!"

"Stop production!" Boris yelled.

Thrilled, Lucia stood up. "That means we get to quit—"

Mr. Mack smiled at her. "That means nothing of the kind. I'm giving you other work to do. Clean this place from top to bottom. And I want the chalkboards and desks and school things put into place. The FBI is coming on Friday to investigate the thumbtack mystery and—"

"The FBI!" Lucia blurted out. "They'll see what you're doing and close you down for good, Mr. Mack. You work us like slaves and you're cruel to the puppies—"

Mr. Mack's neck and face turned an angry red, and the sweep of blond hair above his forehead began to shake. He looked like a long white stick of dynamite about to explode, but he didn't explode. He smiled sweetly. "The FBI is going to find children learning to read and write at the Mack Technical School."

"But this isn't a school."

"We have books and report cards and test scores." Mr. Mack gestured toward a pile of books and papers gathering dust in the corner of the workroom.

"Those are fake and you know it."

"Why don't you just leave then, if you think my school is so horrible?"

Lucia glared at him. Hundreds of Attackaterriers prowled the grounds. There was one safe exit, and Boris unlocked it only when the shift was over.

Mr. Mack laughed and Boris joined in. Then he said, "Scrub the walls, the floors, the ceilings, the tables. Scrub the air." His nostrils flared as he inhaled. "It stinks in here."

"You're not going to get away with it, Mr. Mack," Lucia said.

"Maybe she got a point," Boris whispered.

"I'm not worried about the FBI," Mr. Mack said as he headed back to his office. "I'll charm the FBI into thinking I adore children and puppies."

Lucia tugged on her long black braid. "Well, at least the puppies are safe."

Mr. Mack turned around. "What do you mean?"

"We know what you do over there." She pointed to the Attackaterrier training facility connected by a long corridor to the thumbtack factory. "You stick thumbtacks into their paws to make them mean."

"I do?" Mr. Mack said with a look of false concern. "That does sound cruel."

"Maybe she got another point," Boris whispered. "You can't do the Attacka method of training without thumbtacks."

"True. Puppies need a solid year of my Thumbtack Tactics before they become vicious enough to win the 'Mack's Attackaterrier' seal of approval."

"So," said Lucia brightly. "You can't do any more training, can you?"

The other children grinned.

Mr. Mack scowled at the skinny girl in the center of the crowd. Maybe she led them all in a plot to get rid of the thumbtacks. They certainly looked happy about it. Well, he could change that in a second.

"It's true that I can't do the training today. But I've already ordered a dozen cases of thumbtacks from my competitor. As soon as they arrive and the FBI leaves, I'll be back in business."

Lucia's smile disappeared.

"And don't forget," Mr. Mack warned, "the adult dogs who are guarding this factory are as mean as ever. The training they had when they were puppies is wired into their memory. All the thumbtacks in the world could disappear and they'd still be mean. So don't even think about leaving."

Underneath the surface of the soil, Fip inched along. He had been crawling all night, past colonies of ants, slugs, mites, and fungi, determined to find a home and food for himself. Just because the clan had given up on him didn't mean he would give up. He poked his head through the soil and looked around hopefully.

Unfortunately for him, the Cleveland Park Middle School Environment Club had cleaned the playground. Not a scrap of paper to be found. A lump formed in Fip's throat and his skin prickled.

A voice surprised him from behind. "Who's skinching? You sound too young to be out alone."

Fip turned around to face an enormous blob of a worm. "I'm of the Gamorm Clan," the worm said. "And you?"

"Lumbricus Clan, sort of," said Fip. "I guess I'm looking for a new clan."

"Tank up your gizzard!" said the large worm as it pushed a piece of rotted bark toward Fip. "You sound like you need plumping." The Gamorm worm began chewing on the moldy bark.

Fip wriggled closer, wondering if this Gamorm Clan would take him in. "Smells ummy!" he said, trying to be polite. He sucked up a fleck of the bark rot. "Bluch!" He spit it out and was about to apologize when the air around them darkened. Fip's instincts should have propelled him into the nearest hole. He should have known it was a bird on the lookout for fat, juicy worms. But little Fip didn't go underground. Unfortunately, he screamed and grabbed the fat, juicy worm's rear end.

In a flash, the crow pinched the Gamorm worm in her beak, and before Fip could even think to let go, they were off the ground.

In Mr. Markus Droan's first period science class every seat was full, yet Mr. Droan sat behind his desk calling out the roll. Winny Auster. Here. Randy Butler. Here. Sharmaine Gabott. Here.

Lerner Ghanse sat in the far back corner staring out the large window next to her desk. She had tried pretending she was sick, but her parents didn't buy it. Now she had to face another day and the same dare, which she didn't think was fair. After all, Bobby Nitz had his hawk eyes pinned on her, ready to pounce.

Lerner pushed her bangs out of her eyes and watched the red leaves of a distant maple shake in the strong wind. She'd tell the MPOOEs to forget it. Who needed them? She'd build a cocoon around herself. She'd go underground, become a SLUG. The school year would be over, anyway, in only nine months.

Out of nowhere, a huge crow flew toward Lerner's window. Lerner ducked instinctively, but the crow didn't thump against the glass as she'd expected. Instead, it landed awkwardly on the ledge, gobbled something in its beak, and flew away.

Bobby laughed at Lerner's response. "Did you think it was going to fly in and eat you, Helmet Head?"

As usual, Lerner ignored him. The window was an ancient kind that pushed open from the bottom, and it was open a crack. Lerner reached over to close it and noticed a tiny movement on the white concrete ledge. A bug? A caterpillar? She opened the window more and leaned out for a closer look. A rosy worm, about the length of two rice grains, wriggled toward the window as if trying to find a place to hide. Lerner wasn't crazy about worms, but she didn't like the thought of him being gobbled up by some obnoxious crow.

She picked him up and set him on her desk, next to an article she had cut out of the newspaper.

The little worm was Fip, who had dropped to the ledge the millisecond before the crow had eaten the Gamorm. Now, a tangy whiff flooded Fip's sensors. *Food! Food!* He stretched out and sniffed in wonder at the words of the article laid out before him. A smorgasbord! He skinched onto the paper and began nibbling the nearest thing to his mouth, the letter *J*.

"I suppose no one thought to bring in an article for extra credit," Mr. Droan said.

Lerner raised her hand, forgetting about the worm. "I brought in an article from the *Washington News*," she said, and immediately wished she hadn't. Everyone in the room turned around to stare at her.

After a moment of silence, Mr. Droan raised his bushy eyebrows. "Well, there's a first time for everything. Two points for Ms. Ghanse."

Reba rolled her eyes and Randy snickered.

Sharmaine, the MPOOE who sat in front of Lerner, turned around and whispered helpfully, "Extra credit is not considered cool."

Lerner felt like crawling under a rock.

Mr. Droan handed out work sheets and told them to work quietly. Then he created his usual barricade by propping his grade book on his desk. Behind it, he cracked open a paperback book with a red foil cover (*Burning Heart of Desire*). As he began reading the first page, he reached into his pencil drawer and pulled out a half-empty bag of chocolate chips.

Lerner stared at the work sheet.

Name:_____
Date:_____

Photosynthesis Work Sheet #12
Directions: Copy the definitions for the following plant terms from the book. Write neatly and do your own work!

If she had to be a SLUG in Washington, D.C., why couldn't the classes, at least, be interesting? In history, they did long reports that the teacher didn't bother to grade. In language arts, they didn't read books; so far Ms. Findley just gave spelling tests and handed out grammar work sheets. And they never did any experiments in science. If Lerner didn't see Mr. Droan outside on recess duty, she'd hypothesize that his rear end was chemically bonded to his chair.

She glanced at her newspaper article, which Mr. Droan hadn't even bothered to look at or read. Newspaper articles were more interesting than work sheets. Why couldn't they study real science news?

Lerner imagined herself standing up and ripping the work sheet into confetti. "You call yourself a teacher?" she'd say to Mr. Droan. She imagined all the other students standing up, uniting to demand change.

It would never happen. The MPOOEs were too snobbish and the SLUGs were too spineless. She glanced around the room. Hardly anyone was working. Reba and Randy, the gossip queen and king, were passing notes, probably nasty ones about her. Bobby Nitz was folding his work sheet into a paper airplane, and Julio, an artistic SLUG, was sketching cartoons on his desktop.

Lerner was about to crumple up the article when a small movement caught her eye. That little worm she had rescued was wriggling around. She noticed something—or rather, a lack of something—as he inched to the right. There was a blank space in the article. She peered closer. The worm was hunched down, his body pulsing. Underneath what seemed to be his head, the letter *r* disappeared. The worm curled into a ball and seemed to fall asleep. Lerner looked at the blank space in the article. The words *Jay's Star* had disappeared.

New Star Discovered

TUCSON—A newly dis-
covered star was dubbed
🪱   after the astronomer who found it, Dr.
William Jay. The super-
massive star is expected to
live 5 billion years. Says
Jay, "I've dreamed of this
my whole life."

In a distant galaxy, the reddish light of Jay's Star began to flicker as though a huge breath were trying to blow it out. One second, two seconds, three seconds, and then—*poof!*—the star and its light vanished completely.

In the science classroom, Lerner put the worm in the palm of her hand. He felt rather nice—cool and smooth like Play-Doh. "I've never heard of a worm eating words," she whispered.

She slipped the worm into a neglected terrarium on the shelf next to the window. That should be a safe place for him to live. A little dirt, a few dead leaves. No predators. What more could a worm want?

But saving powerless worms wasn't enough to make Lerner's day bearable. The hours dragged on. During recess she went to the nurse's office with a genuine, Grade-A stomachache. Of course, the MPOOEs would think she was faking it to get out of recess. After school, she deliberately missed the bus so that she wouldn't have to put up with Reba's questions or Bobby's nasty remarks.

Cleveland Park Middle School was in an old neighborhood with big brick houses that were similar to the houses in Lerner's Wisconsin neighborhood. The difference was that the houses here were smooshed up against each other, separated by the skinniest driveways Lerner had ever seen.

She and her best friend, Marie, had always walked to and from school in Wisconsin. Although it was a lot farther to walk here, it felt good to be out in the cool October wind. The maples were already red and the oaks were just turning to gold. Lerner took her time, imagining that she had won a million dollars and was on a shopping trip to buy her own house. By the time she arrived home, she was lost in a fantasy in which Marie had come from Wisconsin to live with her in her new, kids-only mansion.

As she walked up her driveway, Bobby Nitz's Attackaterrier broke the spell by hurling himself against the chain-link fence. Involuntarily, Lerner screamed and was mortified to hear Bobby's bedroom window open.

"Gets you every time, Helmet Head," he yelled, and laughed.

"I don't ever see you playing with Ripper!" Lerner said. "My dad says people shouldn't keep Attackaterriers as pets! He's a vet, you know. And stop calling me Helmet Head."

She was about to go inside when he added, "You don't have to feel scared about going in. Your baby-sitter is already there."

Lerner pushed up her glasses. "She's not my baby-sitter! I don't need a baby-sitter! So mind your own business," she shouted, and slammed the door behind her.

From the family room, Mrs. Chilling yelled, "Save the pieces!" Then, all that could be heard was a man and woman moaning on *Hot Days and Nights,* the TV show that Mrs. Chilling had to watch every day.

In Wisconsin, she didn't need a Mrs. Chilling to be there when she got home from school. In Wisconsin, she and Marie kept each other company.

"You must have been worried when I didn't get off the bus, Mrs. Chilling," Lerner said to herself as she grabbed a handful of cookies from the pantry. "I can see why my mom and dad hired you!" Lerner took a chomp out of a cookie. If she were kidnapped, Mrs. Chilling probably wouldn't even notice.

The family cat slipped into the kitchen and

rubbed against Lerner's leg. She bent down to give her a long stroke. "Hello, good old Martha. How's my fellow prisoner?"

With Martha in one arm and more cookies in the other, Lerner locked herself in her room.

First, she wrote a long letter to Marie. Then, she and Martha curled up on the bed and stared at the ceiling for what seemed like an hour. (Well, Martha fell asleep.) Finally, Lerner got out a pair of scissors and stood up close to the mirror.

"The time has come to take my hair into my own hands, Martha," she announced. She put the scissors in place and made a tiny nip. A massive amount of hair flurried down. She kept cutting across, holding the scissors perfectly, absolutely straight. Then she stepped back to look at the big picture and experienced a near-fatal heart attack. "Oh, Martha! Why didn't you stop me? It looks like an army of naked mole rats chomped across my forehead."

Martha had nothing to say.

Just then, Lerner heard the sound of the front door opening and closing. Her mom and dad were home.

A few minutes later she heard the door again. Mrs. Chilling was going home. After a while, footsteps sounded on the stairs. "Lerner?" Her mom said, and the doorknob jiggled.

"It's locked," Lerner said.

"Well, open it and say hello. I want to hear about your day."

"I'm not coming out until you promise we can move back to Wisconsin," Lerner yelled at the door.

"Honey." Her mother's voice sounded tired. "We can't do that. Your dad and I have new jobs here. You just need more time to get settled. We think this is a wonderful opportunity for all of us."

Wonderful for you, thought Lerner as she pulled on her hair, but not for me.

"Come down when you're ready," her mom said. "We're making chicken and biscuits!"

Five minutes later, Lerner could hear her parents banging around in the kitchen. Cooking was something they all liked to do together. Music started up—an old Beatles' album, which was a favorite of all three—and the banging and clanking got more rhythmic. Lerner could tell her dad was pounding on the flour tub with his wooden spoons. A few seconds later, her mom started wailing along with the chorus. All Lerner had to do was walk down the stairs and she could join in the fun.

Stubbornly, she climbed into bed and put her pillow over her head.

By the time Dr. William Jay arrived at Figer National Observatory, his assistant was already there, looking white in the face. "I have bad news," she said. "Your star disappeared."

Dr. Jay spent the next few hours searching the silent sky with a 10-meter telescope, his mouth hanging open like a black hole.

Wednesday
3
October

"This is a very serious thing. Our worm is completely out of the ordinary."
—E. B. White
Charlotte's Worm

Mr. Droan sat behind his desk, honking out the roll: Winny Auster. Here. Randy Butler. Here. Sharmaine Cabott. Here. When he got to Lerner Chanse, her wish to be absent was so overpowering that she mistakenly said, "Not here."

"If I had that haircut I wouldn't want to be here, either," Queen Reba said.

Everybody laughed.

Lerner pressed her bangs against her forehead. She had heard that the MPOOEs were going to pronounce her a SLUG if she skipped recess again. Lerner's goal of the day was to barf at lunchtime. Right on the table. The nurse would have to send her home. She glanced over at the school lunch menu that was taped on the wall. Today was spinach soufflé. That should do it.

School Lunch Menu

Mon: Corned Beef, Celery
Tues: Spam, Yams
Wed: Spinach Soufflé, Peas
Thurs: Liver, Onions
Fri: Olive Loaf, Zucchini

Mr. Droan started to close his grade book, and Bobby Nitz called out, "I have an extra credit article."

Randy groaned.

"Bring it up," Mr. Droan said.

Bobby walked up and held it out. "It was in this morning's paper. So do I get two points?"

The teacher looked it over without touching it. "Two thousand extra credit points couldn't help your grade, Nitz."

The MPOOEs laughed. Bobby walked back and slammed the paper on his desk.

Lerner couldn't help noticing the headline of his article: JAY'S STAR MISSING. That was odd. The worm had eaten the name of that new star yesterday. Lerner looked over at the terrarium. It took her a while to spot the worm, but when she did she almost fell out of her seat. The worm had grown to the size of three rice grains and was standing up on a twig, wiggling back and forth as if he wanted to catch her attention.

Lerner waited until Mr. Droan handed out the work sheets and submerged behind his grade book, then she pulled the school lunch menu off the board and scooped the worm onto it.

"What are you doing?" Bobby whispered.

"None of your business," Lerner said, and set the paper on her desk. The worm raced over to the nearest word and began to munch. He ate the words *Spinach Soufflé* right off the paper. Then he turned around and lifted his head up at Lerner.

Lerner smiled. "Glad to see you like spinach soufflé. None of us do!" she whispered. "Do you have a name?" She put her thumb on the paper and the worm crawled over. *Fip . . . Fip . . . Fip.* The noise he made as he inched along the paper sounded like a name.

"Fip," Lerner whispered. "What a nice name. I'm Lerner."

Mr. Droan's voice cut through the air. "Ms. Chanse, do you have something you'd like to share with the class?"

"She's talking to a bug," Bobby said.

Everybody turned around to look. Lerner put a cupped hand over Fip and glared at Bobby.

"Get to work, people," Mr. Droan said. His head disappeared behind his propped-up grade book.

Bobby reached over and grabbed the lunch menu off Lerner's desk. Before she could protest, he crumpled it and threw it back at Lerner.

The crumpled ball lay on Lerner's desktop like a wrecked ship. Lerner's heart sank. Nothing as frail and helpless as that baby worm could possibly survive the ordeal. She pretended to work and when no one was looking, carefully opened up the paper. There was Fip, curled up as tight as a peppercorn, dead for sure.

But then he unfurled gracefully and gave a triumphant wriggle. He was alive! Lerner imagined trumpets blaring and herself putting a miniature medal of bravery around his tiny neck.

She waited until class was over, then she put him back in the terrarium.

A buzzer went off. Mrs. Gormano, Cleveland Park Middle School's chief lunch lady, put on her heavy-duty oven mitts. "Spinach soufflés coming out!" she yelled to her assistant and pulled open the monstrous oven door.

Twelve industrial-size pans sat empty in the hot oven.

"What the heck—"

"You forget to make it?" asked Mr. Ryan.

"I filled those pans full!" Mrs. Gormano shook her head. Then she pulled out twelve more drums of spinach, twelve cases of eggs, and twelve gallons of powdered cheese substance. She mixed it all together and poured the slop in the pans.

Everything was fine.

Everything was fine because so far she had a mixture of spinach and eggs and cheese substance. Spinach soufflé only becomes spinach soufflé when it's baked.

Fifty minutes later the buzzer went off, and Mrs. Gormano put on her heavy-duty oven mitts. "Soufflés coming out!" she yelled.

But when she opened the door, the pans were empty again.

Mr. Ryan handed Lerner a lunch tray. Carrot sticks and a peanut butter sandwich.

"What happened to the spinach soufflé?" Lerner asked. She had been trying to work up a nausea.

Mrs. Gormano was sitting near the sink with her large, white-stockinged feet propped up, holding a bag of frozen peas on her forehead. "Don't ask," she said.

"Good," yelled Bobby Nitz from the back of the line. "I hate spinach soufflé."

A strange excitement buzzed in Lerner's chest, and she forgot about her plan to throw up. Did the spinach soufflé really disappear? How? And did all the spinach soufflé in the world disappear or just the soufflé at school? Lerner ate lunch quickly, then got permission to use the pay phone in the foyer. She looked in the yellow pages under *Spinach*. Sal's House of Spinach. That should do. She dialed, and Sal answered.

"Sal's House of Spinach. We got spinach loaf, spinach pie, spinach ice cream. Anything a green lover could want."

Lerner cleared her throat. "What I'd really like is spinach soufflé."

There was a pause. "Well, we usually have soufflé. But something seems to have happened—"

"You have spinach, but no soufflé?"

"Right. Sorry."

Lerner hung up. First Jay's Star and now this. How incredible. The worm must have some kind of magical appetite! Lerner's mind started racing. Could she make him eat the word for something she didn't like, and then would that something disappear? She'd have to experiment. What should she try? She had to get him out of that terrarium. What if she couldn't find him?

She whirled around and smacked into Bobby Nitz.

"What was that phone call about?" he asked.

"Stop bothering me," she said, and stepped around him. She didn't have time for Bobby Nitz. She had to find out more about the worm, and there was only one person in the whole school who would understand. Mrs. Popocheskovich.

The recess bell rang. Lerner ran to the science room and caught Mr. Droan before he went outside. She asked if he'd write her a pass to spend recess in the library doing science research. He stared at her as if she were speaking in Swahili, then wrote out a pass. While he was doing that, she found Fip in the terrarium sleeping under a rock and hid him gently in her closed fist.

When she walked into the library, Mrs. Popocheskovich looked up from the *Improve Your English* book she was reading and smiled. "Hello, Cookie!" the librarian whispered. "Are you feeling so much happy today?"

Lerner smiled back. On the very first day of school, Mrs. Popocheskovich had told Lerner that she was new to Washington, D.C., too. And Lerner liked her from the start. She liked the way she mixed up words in sentences, and the way she wore her paper white hair in an exotic twist on the back of her head, and the way she called her "Cookie." With her accent, it came out sounding like "kooky."

Lerner showed her the pass, and then Fip. "I need a book about worms. I want to find out about this little guy's species. And I need some kind of container to put him in."

"A book about worms. That I would not have guessed," Mrs. Popocheskovich said. She was usually very good at guessing which books her students would like.

The librarian found an old ink bottle and pricked the rubber top a few times. The container was perfect, small enough to fit in Lerner's pocket.

Fip woke up with a start when Lerner dropped him into the bottle, but when he saw her eyeballs through the glass, he relaxed. She was the one who gave him food. She would take care of him. He took one whiff of the residual smell of ink and fell in love with his new home.

Word traveled fast. While Lerner was reading up on worms, the playground was buzzing with the news that she was not going to follow through with the dare. By the time she got to language arts, there was a note waiting on her desk in Reba Silo's handwriting.

> CONGRADULATIONS
> YOUR A SLUG!

Lerner read it over three times. Just this morning, those words had power over her. But now, they seemed silly. Who cared if the MPOOEs called her a SLUG? Lerner had something much more interesting than the MPOOE Club to entertain her: She had magic. Genuine, Grade-A magic. Lerner made a few corrections to Reba's note:

CONGRATULATIONS
YOU'RE A SLUG!

"Sharmaine," Lerner whispered, tapping her on the shoulder with the note. "Pass this back to Reba."

As Sharmaine's hand reached around to grab the note, Mr. Droan looked up.

"Congratulations, Ms. Chanse. You've just earned an after-school detention for you and your friend, Ms. Gabott."

Sharmaine turned and glared.

"I'm sorry!" Lerner said. Of all the MPOOEs, Sharmaine was the one Lerner was hoping would become her friend.

"Lerner is NOT Sharmaine's friend, Mr. Droan," Reba announced.

"Thank you so much for that important news flash," Mr. Droan said.

Lerner reddened. Reba still had some power over her.

After school, Bobby went to the library and called up the online edition of the news to see if there was any news about spinach soufflé. He typed the words into the search command field, and a new article materialized on his screen.

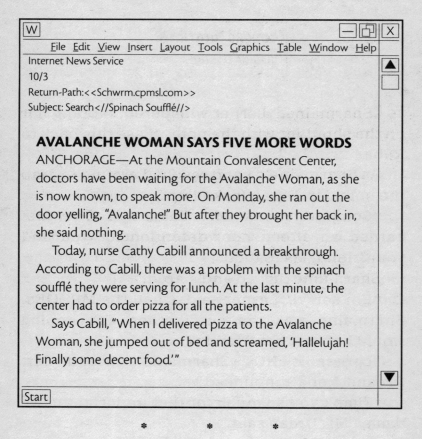

W   — ⬜ X

File   Edit   View   Insert   Layout   Tools   Graphics   Table   Window   Help

Internet News Service

10/3

Return-Path:<<Schwrm.cpmsl.com>>

Subject: Search<//Spinach Soufflé//>

AVALANCHE WOMAN SAYS FIVE MORE WORDS

ANCHORAGE—At the Mountain Convalescent Center, doctors have been waiting for the Avalanche Woman, as she is now known, to speak more. On Monday, she ran out the door yelling, "Avalanche!" But after they brought her back in, she said nothing.

Today, nurse Cathy Cabill announced a breakthrough. According to Cabill, there was a problem with the spinach soufflé they were serving for lunch. At the last minute, the center had to order pizza for all the patients.

Says Cabill, "When I delivered pizza to the Avalanche Woman, she jumped out of bed and screamed, 'Hallelujah! Finally some decent food.'"

Start

*   *   *

"Welcome to after-school detention, Ms. Chanse and Ms. Cabott," Mr. Droan said. "You may sit on opposite sides of the room and contemplate the errors of your ways."

Lerner sat down and smiled. Finally, some quiet time to think about this whole thing with Fip.

"Do you think this is amusing, Ms. Chanse?" asked Mr. Droan.

Lerner pressed her lips together. Mr. Droan snorted and tucked his hands under his armpits. Leaning back in his chair, he dozed off. Quietly, Lerner pulled out Fip's ink bottle and put her head down on her desk so that she could stare eye to eye with him.

She tried to think through what she knew and what she didn't know about this little creature. He ate the words *spinach soufflé* and spinach soufflé disappeared, but not spinach. If he had just eaten the word *spinach,* would all spinach have disappeared? She smiled at the thought, then a little shiver crawled up her spine. Could the magic be that far-reaching? If Fip had eaten the word *stars* instead of *Jay's Star* would all the stars in the world have disappeared? Lerner tried to imagine a sky without any stars. If the magic was that strong, she'd have to be very careful about what she let him eat.

Vaguely, she remembered teachers complaining on Monday about thumbtacks that had disappeared. Was Fip responsible for that?

Fip stretched, and the simple shape and small size of his body hit Lerner like a reality check. I'm crazy, Lerner thought. An itsy-bitsy worm couldn't have the power to make things disappear, could it? She had to do an experiment. She emptied out her backpack to see what word or words she could give him to eat.

 No. She wouldn't want flavor to disappear.

 Movies! Forget it. She loved them.

Her pocket calendar caught her eye. What about a number? What would happen then? What about a whole date? Could a day disappear? Lerner thought about the day her parents loaded her into the moving van, the day her father closed the door on their wonderful old yellow house in Wisconsin. September 1. That was a day Lerner would like to erase.

Lerner's heart pounded. That was it! She'd let Fip eat September 1. If that day never occurred, then her parents wouldn't have moved and she'd beam back in time to her old house.

Before she could change her mind, she shook Fip out of his bottle. She had already torn out the page for September, but there was a mini calendar for the whole year on the back page. She set him on the number *1* under September.

Fip sniffed it. Hesitantly, he took a bite out of the bottom of the number. Crunchly! Crunchly! Much different from a letter. Jaws working, he crunched the rest of the number. How would he describe it? Oaky with a smatch of iron.

Lerner picked him up, her hand shaking. Was it nervousness or was something magical happening? It felt like a swarm of hornets were migrating from her stomach to her heart. She closed her eyes. Was she moving? Was something happening?

She opened her eyes, and there was Mr. Droan with his eyes still closed, itching his eyebrow with a pinkie. She looked down at the calendar. The date was gone. Something magical should have happened. Then, she noticed that it was next year's calendar, not this year's.

Year At-A-Glance

AUGUST

S	M	T	W	T	F	S
				1	2	3
4	5	6	7	8	9	10
11	12	13	14	15	16	17
18	19	20	21	22	23	24
25	26	27	28	29	30	31

SEPTEMBER

S	M	T	W	T	F	S
	2	3	4	5	6	7
8	9	10	11	12	13	14
15	16	17	18	19	20	21
22	23	24	25	26	27	28
29	30					

Oh great! What did that mean? What would happen next September? She wanted to change the past, but she wasn't so sure about messing with the future. Would the world lose a day? *Could* the world lose a day? Lerner's stomach turned. Did she just do something terrible? She'd have to wait a long time to find out. Why had she been so reckless? She needed to pick something uncomplicated to try. Something she could see.

Mr. Droan stood up and stretched. A button popped off his shirt and rolled across the room. "All right, girls. Detention is over."

Lerner stuffed everything in her backpack, ran out the door and down the long, empty hallway. She had missed the bus, so she was going to have to walk again. Good. It would give her time to think. Her mind was spinning. As she raced down the hall, she noticed every word of every sign, poster, and label. For the first time, she was aware of how much print there was in the world, and she was aware of not just the words, but also the realities that the words represented. EXIT. FIRE ALARM. PRINCIPAL. LIBRARY. WELCOME KINDERGARTNERS! KOPPY DRINKING FOUNTAIN SYSTEMS. LEAD-FREE!

She stopped in front of the vending machine in the foyer and looked at all the candy bars hanging from their metal hooks inside the glass. Giggle Bar. Nutty Munch. Goo Choo. Then she noticed a small white tag glued to the machine.

VENDING MACHINE NO. 203

Lerner glanced around. The hallway was still empty. On impulse, she shook Fip out and placed him on the label.

Dizzy, Fip gripped the label tightly with his bristles. So much rustle bustle in one day! He'd been hoisted up and down and almost smooshed. Now he was expected to eat sideways! He sniffed the V. Not too fresh, but not bad. Steadily, he ate every letter and the crunchlies.

* * *

47

Lerner plucked him off and took a step back. Nothing happened for a moment, then the machine started to shimmer. One, two, three seconds . . . and the vending machine vanished. Rows of candy bars and a massive pile of quarters hung in midair for a split second, then hit the floor.

Lerner yelped. She looked around and saw Sharmaine at the other end of the hall coming her way. Quickly she put Fip back in the bottle, then began stuffing candy bars and quarters into her backpack, a smile spreading from ear to ear. Incredible! She felt like Santa Claus loading a sack full of goodies. Ho! Ho! Ho! She had magic power in her grasp. How did she get so lucky?

Sharmaine's footsteps slowed as she got nearer. Lerner stood up, hands full with candy bars. She piled the candy on top of the books in Sharmaine's arms, laughed, and said, "Merry Christmas from a SLUG!" Hoisting her own pack over one shoulder, she ran out the door.

Thursday
4
October

"I think I have got it in me to be a saint of some kind."
—Sue Townsend
The Secret Diary of Adrian Worm

At the Cleveland Park Middle School, Principal Eve Norker's voice came booming over the intercom system into Mr. Droan's room. "There has been a serious theft. It occurred sometime after school yesterday. The police are looking into it. I sincerely hope no students were involved."

The principal's announcement flew in one of Lerner's ears and out the other. For the fifth time since she got off the bus, Lerner checked the side pocket of her backpack. Nestled amid a dozen candy bars, Fip's ink bottle was still there.

Mrs. Norker continued. "The stolen vending machine was . . ."

The words screeched to a halt in the listen-to-me section of Lerner's brain. VENDING MACHINE! Mrs. Norker was talking about Vending Machine No. 203! The one Fip had made disappear. Lerner glanced out of the corner of her eye to see if anyone was looking at her. Just then, Sharmaine turned around, eyes wide with surprise.

Would Sharmaine tell the police that Lerner had been at the scene of the crime? That she had walked off with candy bars and quarters?

Somehow Lerner didn't think Sharmaine was the type to tattle. But even if she did, nobody could prove a thing. Besides, Lerner didn't steal the vending machine. Fip was really the one directly responsible for the disappearance of the machine. What would the police do . . . arrest a worm? Lerner imagined little Fip on trial in a courtroom, putting his bristles on the Bible and saying, I swear to tell the truth and nothing but the truth . . .

Mr. Droan's voice brought Lerner back to reality. "All right, people. Clear your desks," he said. "It's test time."

Lerner's stomach sank. Instead of studying, she'd spent the night eating Goo Choos and making a mental list of words she'd like to feed Fip:

1. Tooth decay
2. Fractions and long division
3. Wool (she was allergic)
4. *Hot Days and Nights* (the annoying television show Mrs. Chilling had to watch at 3:30 every day)
5. Dust (her mother was allergic)
6. Mad Cow disease and any other horrible animal infections (her father was a veterinarian)
7. Airplane fares (then everyone could ride for free and she could fly back to Wisconsin every weekend)

The list went on, and although making it had been fun, it had been stupid not to review the chapter. Mr. Droan's tests were duplicates of the "sample tests" in the book, so if you just took a minute to look at the chapter before the test, you could pass with no problem.

"Ms. Chanse. Backpack under your chair now."

Reluctantly, Lerner took a pencil out and was just about to set her backpack under her desk when she had an idea. She tucked Fip in her hand and put her pack away.

Fip rubbed his underbelly bristles together.

He'd spent the night replaying the vanishing vending machine scene over and over in his mind. He didn't know how or why, but he knew that he was the reason that huge machine disappeared. Hungry and excited to see exactly what he was capable of doing, he skinched around and around in Lerner's cupped hand until she giggled.

Mr. Droan frowned and gave a huge stack of exams to Winny the SLUG to pass out. "I would wish you luck, but luck isn't going to save you now," he said.

Nonchalantly, Lerner put her palm down next to the test's title. Fip plopped out gracefully and sniffed.

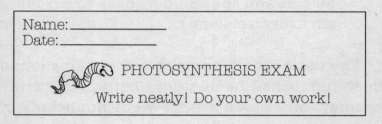

Name:_____
Date:_____

PHOTOSYNTHESIS EXAM
Write neatly! Do your own work!

Her classmates scribbled away while Lerner watched Fip nibble the letter *P*. She bit her lip to keep from smiling.

"Lerner Chanse, stop daydreaming and get busy," Mr. Droan said and ducked behind his propped-up grade book to read the final chapter of *Burning Heart of Desire*.

Careful not to smoosh Fip, Lerner wrote her name at the top. Growing more robust and agile every day, Fip munched away like a tiny deleting machine. He'd already finished eating the words PHOTOSYNTHESIS and was almost done with EXAM.

Please work. Lerner closed her eyes. *Please work.* When she opened her eyes, Mr. Droan's exam on photosynthesis was shimmering just as the vending machine had. Out of the corner of her eye, she saw more shimmering. It wasn't just her exam. All the tests were shimmering.

To Fip, the magic felt like an earthquake. The paper underneath him was splitting apart, molecule by molecule, each part vibrating wildly. He screamed and waved his bristles.

Entranced by the shimmering light, Lerner didn't even notice him.

One second . . .

Two seconds . . .

"Hey," whispered Bobby. "What's going on . . ."

Three seconds.

Fip hit the nicely solid wood of Lerner's desktop. The paper was completely gone. Lerner looked around. All the desktops in the room were empty. The room was dead silent.

Lost in *Burning Heart of Desire,* Mr. Droan had forgotten that his students even existed.

"Uh—Mr. Droan . . . ," Reba said. "The tests . . ."

Mr. Droan looked up and blinked at the empty desks. "Very funny. Ha. Ha. Get back to work."

No one spoke.

"This is very simple, people," Mr. Droan said. "Put your tests back on your desk and get to work."

Everybody started talking at once.

Lerner put a cupped hand over the exhausted Fip and tried to look calm. Inside her head, her own voice was shooting off like a firecracker: *Fip has magic power! And I have Fip!* It was the most incredible thing that had ever happened to her, the most incredible thing that had ever happened to anybody.

Mr. Droan frowned, his eyebrows smashing together. "Bobby—"

"Don't look at me!" Bobby said.

Mr. Droan whirled around to face Reba. "Ms. Silo, does this have anything to do with your little club?"

Well, this accusation was startling. Teachers had generally thought the MPOOE Club was cute—an impression Reba had worked hard to maintain. Now, the club was actually being linked to something bad that they didn't even do! Reba stammered that she didn't know anything, and the sound of her faltering voice made many of the MPOOEs in the room take pause.

Lerner grinned. She felt like standing up and

shouting, "Now who's the Most Powerful One On Earth?"

"Ms. Chanse, you look like you're enjoying yourself. Perhaps you know something about this?"

Lerner's smile vanished. She shrugged, avoiding Mr. Droan's eyes.

"All right, people," the teacher said. "You all have after-school detention today and every day until the tests are returned."

The class groaned.

"This is not excellent," Reba muttered darkly.

Sharmaine turned around and looked under Lerner's desk as if she expected to find the tests in a neat pile under Lerner's feet.

"My mom is going to kill me!" Winny the SLUG sobbed. "I've never had detention!"

A ping of guilt hit Lerner, but she ponged it away by remembering that she hadn't *intended* to get everybody in trouble. Winny was exaggerating. After-school detention wasn't even that big of a deal. And Mr. Droan couldn't keep them in detention forever, could he?

By lunchtime, the whole school was buzzing. Mr. Droan told the principal that someone had stolen the exams, and the principal made everyone who was in Droan's first-period science class spend recess sitting in the lunchroom. The students were confused and furious—especially the MPOOEs.

During Ms. Findley's fifth period language arts class, Reba and Randy passed notes to everyone.

MPOOEs rule this school. Nothing happens without MPOOE approval. Whoever did this we will find you. No one gets us in trouble.

The threat scared many a SLUG, even though they hadn't done a thing. Bobby responded to his note by folding it into an ultralight glider and hitting the back of Reba's head with it when Ms. Findley wasn't looking.

Lerner had to laugh. She should have been scared by the announcement, but she wasn't. Nothing could bother her. Who cared about after-school detention? If you were Lerner Chanse, you could feed the word *detention* to Fip and it would disappear! Not a bad idea, Lerner thought. Maybe I'll do that tomorrow.

Altogether, it turned out to be an amazing day for Lerner. Her last class, history, went to the library to work on their "Everyday Life in Colonial America" reports. She got her favorite carrel in the back and tried to concentrate on her report, but every time she read a word she imagined what would happen if Fip were to eat it. *Cotton. Tea. Stockings. Firewood. Ink!*

About five minutes into the period, Sharmaine, who was sitting in the next carrel, leaned over and whispered, "I won't tell the MPOOEs. You had something to do with the vending machine and the tests, didn't you?" Her voice was sincere and nicely conspiratorial; there was something in it Lerner wanted to trust.

The thing was—Lerner liked her. Sharmaine didn't put people down the way Reba did. And Sharmaine wrote genuine, Grade-A poems in a spiral notebook, which Lerner often read over her shoulder during Mr. Droan's science class. Lerner also kept a secret journal, which she would consider showing to Sharmaine, if Sharmaine were her friend. The problem was— Sharmaine was a MPOOE. And she couldn't trust a MPOOE.

"Knowledge is power," Lerner gloated. "I have it, and the MPOOEs don't."

Mrs. Popocheskovich rolled by with her cart full of books, and Sharmaine ducked back in her own carrel. The librarian shelved a book and leaned in toward Lerner. "It was Francis Bacon who said that knowledge is power, Cookie," she whispered. "He was a philosopher who said much things to make you run and think. He also said that the appetite for too much power caused the angels to fall." The librarian patted her twist and pushed her cart to the next aisle.

In the quiet of the library, Lerner thought about what Mrs. Popocheskovich said. Knowledge about Fip was an awesome power. Power that Lerner could use for good—or evil. She shouldn't waste the power on childish things like vending machines and tests—although that had been fun. Fip was a gift to be used for the good of humankind. With a new sense of purpose and righteous excitement, she borrowed a copy of the *Washington News* and scanned through it for ideas.

CRIME ON RISE
JAPAN ROCKED BY EARTHQUAKES

The newspaper was filled with life-and-death matters. Lerner imagined feeding Fip the word *crime* and watching murder weapons vanish. *Ta Da!* She imagined feeding Fip the word *earthquake* and calming a fault line in mid-tremble. *Hurray!* She could do it. She had the power.

Or did she? What if Fip only had a certain amount of power and it was almost gone? Lerner didn't know that much about Fip, after all. The books on invertebrates that she had borrowed yesterday were no help. Fip didn't look or act like any of the worms described. All she knew was what Fip had done, not what he was capable of doing in the future. Perhaps he was a completely new—or alien?—species. She'd do more experiments and keep track of her findings in her journal. She needed to stick to things that she could see. *Crime* and *earthquake* were too big: What if the desire to commit a crime is what disappeared? How could she see that? And how could she find out whether or not she had stopped an earthquake from happening?

She needed something specific, a name that only referred to one very immediate thing, something she could see. She needed—what did Ms. Findley call it?—a proper noun. She turned the page and an article caught her eye.

ATTACKATERRIER BITES BABY

DENVER—An Attackaterrier attacked another toddler. City officials voted to require the fierce breed of dog to be muzzled and chained at all times.

Dog experts agree that there is something about the way Attackaterriers are trained that makes them dangerous. "Attackaterriers give dogs a bad name," says Sandy Scooper, National Pet Owners Association. "I'm not sure what Mr. Mack does to produce such vicious dogs, but we do not recommend them as pets. You can't *play* with an Attackaterrier."

Archibald Mack of Mack Industries refused to comment.

Attackaterriers. That was it! She could delete Attackaterriers. Life without Ripper flashed before her eyes. Imagine! She and Martha could frolic in their own backyard without the constant growling. Good old Martha could become an outdoor cat again.

Although Lerner should have been writing her "Everyday Life in Colonial America" report, she pulled out her journal and wrote plans for the next experiment:

```
                    Lerner Chanse
    Experiment

    Fip will eat this word: Attackaterriers

    Hypothesis: All Attackaterriers will disappear.

    Results:
```

She could do it after school in her bedroom and see right through her window if it worked on Ripper. She couldn't wait, but she had to. After history class, she had to report to Mr. Droan's room for detention along with everybody else.

The room was packed. Lerner sat in her usual place in the back and pretended to do her homework. The MPOOEs were up to something, passing notes up and down the rows—to MPOOE members only—like a hive of worker bees. Queen Reba sat in the center with her chest sticking out as usual, watching every move.

The top of Mr. Droan's head appeared and

disappeared behind his propped-up grade book with every snore.

Lerner looked over Sharmaine's shoulder. She couldn't see the note Reba had passed her, but she could see the poem Sharmaine had just written in her spiral notebook.

> More trouble than it's worth
> Possibly the worst club on earth
> Only filled with twits
> One day soon, I'll quit
> Escape! Escape! Before it's too late!

Now this was an interesting development.

Lerner opened her backpack and pulled out a Nutty Munch. As she took a bite, she felt Winny the SLUG's perfectly round eyes on her. Feeling powerful in a saintly kind of way, Lerner pulled out another Nutty Munch and handed it to Winny, who grinned and straightened up in her seat. Lerner glanced at the kids in the room who weren't wearing MPOOE wristbands. Then she, the Good Deed Doer, pulled out a dozen Nutty Munches. *For SLUGs only* she wrote on each wrapper. One by one, she passed them to all the SLUGs. Well, all but Bobby Nitz.

She slipped a note around the last Nutty Munch and passed it to Sharmaine.

> You are hereby invited to become a SLUG.

The MPOOEs watched silently. Reba looked like she wanted to spit thumbtacks. Bobby pretended not to notice.

School was getting fun.

After detention, Bobby Nitz ran out the door and kept running, fast and hard, until it felt as though his lungs would burst. He hated school. He hated Droan and he hated the other kids. He hated Helmet Head with her stupid candy bars for SLUGs only. He slowed to a walk, the concrete sidewalk slamming up through his thin-soled sneakers. He wished he could run so fast that his feet would leave the ground. He wished his bones were hollow like a bird's so he could fly. He'd fly above Thirty-sixth Street, past the turnoff to his house, past the parkway and the zoo. He'd fly and fly and keep on flying, out of town, out of the world.

Ahead, the stoplight turned red. He pounded right into the intersection, and a car screeched to a stop, honking. The driver got out to yell, and Bobby took off running again, plowing past a group of third graders on the corner who were too scared to protest. When he got home, he ran straight to his father's den and locked the door.

He turned on the computer and called up the Internet.

Outside, Ripper barked. Somebody screamed. Bobby parted his window curtain and looked out. Helmet Head. She was in the driveway walking over to Ripper's pen, closer than Bobby had ever seen her dare to come. Staying hidden, he eased the window a crack.

"That's the last time you're going to scare me." Lerner was talking to Ripper. "I've got a little surprise for you named Fip."

Every cell in Bobby's brain came to attention. What did she mean—a surprise named Fip? Bobby saw her flash a smile at Ripper and walk into her house. No way! Lerner Chanse never smiled at Ripper. The image of Lerner riding on a broomstick with her short blond hair sticking straight up flew in and out of Bobby's mind. Maybe she wasn't a witch, but odd things were happening and she was involved. It all started with the thumbtacks, which he got when he slammed into her. She brought in an article about Jay's Star, and the next day the star disappeared. Then, she used the lunch menu to hold some bug, and the spinach soufflé disappeared. A bunch of coincidences? No way! Today the principal talked about the missing vending machine, and guess who was passing out candy bars like a millionaire? And Lerner was smiling when Droan's tests disappeared. That was definitely odd.

Bobby got his binoculars and tried to see into Lerner's bedroom window. What was going on? And what was this surprise named Fip? No luck. Her curtains were drawn.

Turning back to the computer, he typed in "vending machine."

```
┌────────────────────────────────────────────────┐
│ W                                    ─  ⊡  X     │
├────────────────────────────────────────────────┤
│   File  Edit  View  Insert  Layout  Tools  Graphics  Table  Window  Help │
├────────────────────────────────────────────────┤
│ Internet News Service                        ▲  │
│ 10/4                                         □  │
│ Return-Path:<<R.mNitz.cd.com>>                  │
│ Subject: Search<//Vending Machine//>            │
│                                                 │
│ VENDOR HEARTBROKEN                              │
│ WASHINGTON, D.C. Brian Coleberg loved Vending   │
│ Machine Number 203. "Number 203 was a particular│
│ beauty," says Coleberg with a tear in his eye.  │
│     Coleberg's machine was stolen from Cleveland Park │
│ Middle School this week. Police have no clues.  │
│     "I don't understand why anyone would do this to Mr. │
│ Coleberg," says CPMS Principal Eve Norker. "We ordered the │
│ machine from him because he's an honest, kind man." │
│                                              ▼  │
├────────────────────────────────────────────────┤
│ Start                                           │
└────────────────────────────────────────────────┘
```

*   *   *

Lerner ran in the back door, holding her backpack tightly against her chest.

Martha met her at the door with a meow.

"Hello, good old Martha!" Lerner scooped up her cat. "Come on up to my room! I'm going to do a little experiment that I think you'll like."

"Stop right there, young lady," Mrs. Chilling said with a sour smile on her face. "I have three messages for you. Number one: The school called your mother at work to inform her of your detentions! Number two: Your mother called here to get an explanation! And number three: You're grounded until further notice!"

Lerner looked at Mrs. Chilling's pursed lips. You're enjoying this, aren't you, Mrs. Chilling? she said to herself. She took Martha up to her room where the cat climbed onto her desk and settled down for a nap.

Lerner sighed. She wished Marie were here. Marie would help her figure out what to say to her parents. She sat at her desk and started spilling her guts.

Dear Marie,
I miss you. You won't believe what is happening here. I found this magic worm, at least I think he's a worm. And I'm afraid that if I tell my parents, they'll take him away. His name is Fip and he's red orange and . . .

Lerner shook Fip out of his ink bottle and set him on the top of her desk so that she could get a good look before describing him to Marie.

Fip took one whiff of good old Martha and his gizzard practically turned inside out. He screamed and curled into a ball.

Martha blinked and twitched her whiskers, but she didn't bother getting up.

"Sorry, Martha, I think he's scared of you." Lerner scooped up her old cat and put her in the hallway.

Fip took a quick breath in and glanced around to get his bearings. Ever since that earthquake, he was on edge. But, ah! A tangy whiff! There was a piece of paper with quite a bit of food on it. Lerner's attention was calm and focused toward him, which made him feel calm, too. He liked the vibrations he felt when she paid attention to him. He skinched closer to her hand, and she smiled.

Fip had grown plumper now, about the size of a large buttonhole, and was looking more like a caterpillar than a worm to Lerner. He had the cutest way of scrunching up the middle part of his body when he crawled. He was really quite remarkable, with delicate lines around his body, and when he chewed, his whole body trembled. Fascinated, Lerner watched him, and then realized with horror that he was eating the letter *M* in "Marie." She screamed and grabbed him. Just then, the sound of barking came through the window.

Ripper! She had forgotten about her plan to delete Attackaterriers.

Lerner looked out her window just in time to see Ripper killing a bird. She opened her journal. Attackaterriers. All she had to do was set Fip down on the word, and she could make Attackaterriers history.

"What do you think, Fip? Should we do it?"

Martha meowed at the door.

"Not now, Martha!"

Lerner thought about her cat and started losing her nerve. Ripper wasn't a pet to the Nitzes, but what if someone somewhere loved an Attackaterrier the way she loved Martha?

Outside the window Ripper growled. An idea came to her. She wouldn't delete all Attackaterriers. She'd just delete Ripper! She wrote out a new experiment and set Fip down near the *R*.

Lerner Chanse

Experiment

Fip will eat this word: Attackaterriers

Hypothesis: All Attackaterriers will disappear.

Results:

Fip will eat these words:

Ripper, the Attackaterrier

Hypothesis: Just Ripper will disappear

Results:

Fip looked at her, trying to figure things out. Just a moment ago her alarm chemicals filled the air when she saw him eat. Now she wanted him to eat. It was confusing!

"Come on, Fip," Lerner said.

Fip sniffed the *R*. It was hard to resist such an ummy snack.

Lerner grabbed the binoculars hanging in her closet. As soon as Fip finished eating the last little curl of the last letter, she put him into his ink bottle and looked out the window. In the Nitzes' backyard, Ripper's body began to shimmer. He opened his mouth and a yelp wobbled out. One, two, three seconds . . . then the dog pen was empty.

Completely empty.

So empty that it gave Lerner a little chill. What had she just done? An uneasy feeling crept into her stomach.

The Nitzes' car pulled up with Mr. and Mrs. Nitz in it. Lerner froze. Oh great! The one time they come home from work early has to be today.

They got out, hoisting fat briefcases. According to Lerner's dad, Mr. Robert Nitz, Sr., was a very important prosecutor who put countless criminals in jail, and Mrs. Nitz was a very important flower arranger who arranged flowers for dinner parties at the White House. They always looked very important, Lerner supposed. But she didn't like them. Mrs. Nitz was too quiet, and Mr. Nitz was too loud.

"Where the devil is that dog?" Mr. Nitz was asking as they headed inside.

Lerner held her breath. A moment later he came out with Bobby.

"All right," Mr. Nitz said. "You show me where he is."

Bobby looked at the empty pen. "He's . . . he was—"

"You're an imbecile! Do you know how much that dog cost?"

"But I didn't let him out—"

"I suppose the dog let himself out?"

"I don't know how—"

"You know what's going to happen? That dog is going to kill somebody, and I'll get sued." Mr. Nitz slammed the gate. "Robert Nitz getting sued! Imagine that one! You're going to pay for this, Bobby!"

"But I didn't let him—"

Mr. Nitz wheeled around to face his son. "You can't do anything right, you know that?"

Bookworm's Desk Calendar

Friday
5
October

"Beware!" squeaked the magic talking
mice in the walls.
—Edworm Eager
Half Magic

At 8:00 A.M., Lerner got on the school bus with
Fip in her backpack and a hat pulled over her
head.

About fifteen kids were already on the bus, a
few MPOOEs, a few SLUGs, and some kids from

other grades. Randy stood up from his usual seat in the center and looked beyond her. "Where's Nitz?" he wanted to know.

Another MPOOE jumped up and peered out at the Nitzes' house. "If he's absent, it won't be as good."

"Shut up," hissed Reba.

The bus driver yelled at everybody to sit down, yanked the doors shut, and pulled out.

Lerner's stomach was in knots. What were the MPOOEs plotting? And where was Bobby? She felt horribly guilty about Ripper. Mr. Nitz's words kept playing over and over in her head. She couldn't imagine her parents talking to her that way.

Her parents had been angry about the detentions, but they didn't call her names. They gave her a nice long lecture about behavior and how important it was to make a good impression at school. Usually, she hated lectures, but after hearing Mr. Nitz yell at Bobby, she didn't think her parents' lectures were so bad.

She had made a horrible mistake deleting Ripper. It was absolutely wrong to delete something living. She definitely was *not* going to go through with the Attackaterrier experiment.

The bus rumbled over a pothole. Sharmaine turned around and looked at her. For a second, Lerner thought she was going to declare herself a SLUG. But then Sharmaine looked away.

Reba moved to an empty seat next to Lerner. "So, where did you get all those Nutty Munches yesterday, SLUG?"

The bus turned a wide corner, rolling on and off the curb with elephant-like thumps. She turned to Reba calmly and said, "My name is Lerner, not SLUG."

Lerner saw Sharmaine smile.

"I have an excellent idea," Reba went on. "Why don't you open your backpack and let me see if you've got any more candy in there."

"Forget it." Lerner pulled her backpack in. "You're just mad because I gave them to SLUGs. You can't tell me what to do, Reba."

"I'm just worried about you, Lerner. I think you might have stolen those candy bars and I don't want you to get into trouble."

The bus rumbled over another pothole. Lerner kept quiet, hoping Reba would go back to her seat.

"So, where's neighbor boy?" Reba asked.

"I don't keep track of Bobby."

Reba glared. "There's something going on. We think both you and Nitz are in on it. You have both been acting strange. And we're going to find out what it is. Just wait till you see what we have planned for Nitz."

The bus pulled into the school parking lot. What did they mean they have something planned for Bobby, Lerner wondered. Now what?

At 8:45 A.M., the Mack Technical School on Bellitas Island was ready. The children were sitting at their tables, penmanship books open on their desks, newly sharpened pencils poised. Fake test scores were taped onto the bulletin board. Boris, the bodyguard, was sitting on a stool at a large chalkboard pretending to be a teacher, scratching under his collar as if his fancy suit gave him hives.

Mr. Mack surveyed the scene. The FBI investigator was due to arrive any moment. There was only one thing left to do, Mr. Mack thought, get rid of that skinny girl with the big mouth.

As if she could read his mind, Lucia spoke up, "Shouldn't we be writing something in these notebooks?"

Boris looked at Mr. Mack. "She got a point, Boss."

"Fine. Fine," Mr. Mack said, as he walked the floor. "Write 'See Spot Run' on the board and everyone can copy it."

Lucia went to the board and wrote:

Frio Re Bampas.

Anybody who speaks Bellitan knows that Frio Re Bampas does not mean See Spot Run. It means: Free the Children. And when Lucia wrote the revolutionary statement on the board, all the children in the room straightened up in their seats.

Lucia looked out at her friends with a stone face, willing them to keep their cool. She could see the questions in their eyes: What was she up to? Would Mr. Mack catch on?

Mr. Mack was staring hard at the writing, unwilling to admit that he didn't know Bellitan. "Write it in English, too," he finally said.

Underneath the Bellitan words, Lucia wrote:

See Spot Run.

"Does that look right?" Mr. Mack whispered to Boris, who shrugged. Mr. Mack walked over to the youngest kid in the factory, a baby-faced eight-year-old. "Is that right?"

Lucia stared at the boy, praying he wouldn't crack. To his credit, the little boy nodded and smiled.

Mr. Mack told all the children to copy the letters in their books, and he grabbed Lucia's arm. "You come with me."

She rooted her feet to the floor and scrutinized his face with unblinking eyes. "Where to?"

"You little—" Mr. Mack swallowed the scream rising in his throat, realizing that it wouldn't do to get angry. "I found a box of books we should be using. You can distribute them."

Lucia pulled her arm away and followed him out the double doors. As they walked down the long hallway, Lucia kept her eyes peeled, suspicious. They stopped at a door labeled:

STORAGE

"Here we are," Mr. Mack said. He punched a code into a small box on the side of the door, and the lock clicked open. "You'll find a box of books to the right of the door. Just bring it back to the factory." He smiled, and before Lucia could object, he pushed her inside.

The door slammed shut, and Mr. Mack laughed. He pulled the fake sign off the door and stuck the real one back on.

BEWARE OF DOGS

---

*   *   *

Lerner had five minutes before the first bell rang, so she ran to the sanctuary of the library. There was Bobby Nitz hunched at the computer. He had obviously come to school early, probably avoiding the whole bus scene. She was relieved to see that he was okay. Overnight, she'd dreamed up some terrible scenarios in which he was driven away by his angry father. Anyway, it was all her imagination. He looked perfectly fine—his feet jiggling under his chair as usual.

She stood for a moment noticing his mud-caked shoes, his untied laces, and saw how alone he was. To be a SLUG was bad enough, but to be Bobby Nitz had to be the worst. At least SLUGs had the potential to make friends with other SLUGs; nobody wanted to make friends with Bobby. He was the first one everybody suspected of doing something wrong. Because of her, the MPOOEs were planning something against him. It wasn't right. It was like his dad blaming him for Ripper's disappearance. She should warn him about the MPOOEs. That was the right thing to do. So how come she wasn't doing it?

"Good morning, Cookie." Mrs. Popocheskovich emerged from her office holding a cup of coffee and a stack of newspapers. "How's that worm book?"

"Not too helpful," Lerner said. "I think the worm I found hasn't been written about yet."

Mrs. Popocheskovich smiled. "You maybe discovered a new species, eh?"

Lerner nodded. An idea was worming its way into her mind. Maybe it was the guilt, but she couldn't stop thinking about Bobby. He had nothing. She didn't exactly have a hundred new friends, but she did have Marie to write to. And at home, there were her parents and good old Martha. Every person should have something good in his life—even Bobby Nitz. She wished that instead of getting rid of Ripper, she could have made him less vicious.

That was it!

"Mrs. Popocheskovich," she said with growing excitement. "Do you know how Attackaterriers become Attackaterriers?"

Mrs. Popocheskovich set her papers down. "From worms to dogs. Lerner, what is sitting on that brain of yours?"

"Haven't you ever noticed the ads?" Lerner picked up a newspaper and leafed through it until she saw an Attackaterrier advertisement. "See!" She pointed to the ad. "They get mean by some 'Attacka' method. So what if you could take the 'Attacka' out of Attackaterrier. What would you have left?"

"Terriers?"

"Yes! And that would be great, wouldn't it?"

"Well, I must admit I feel bad for those dogs. They don't look like they're having so much happy, if you know what I'm saying."

Lerner grinned. "Thanks, Mrs. Popocheskovich!"

"You're so much welcome," the librarian smiled. "But for what did I do?"

Lerner hurried past Bobby to her carrel in the back. She pulled out her experiment notebook and wrote a new experiment.

She set Fip down on the letter *A*. "Here's a little breakfast," she whispered, and then thought to herself that it wasn't little at all.

Lucia was hit with blinding sunlight and a horrible stench at the same time. She blinked, covering her mouth and nose. She was outside. But where? And why did Mr. Mack push her out here?

She looked down. That's where the smell came from! She had stepped right into a pile of dog poop. A sick feeling crept into her stomach. She looked up, her eyes adjusting to the light.

Twenty pairs of eyes met hers. Yellow eyes. Attackaterrier eyes.

Every muscle froze. She knew where she was. She was inside one of the large Attackaterrier pens in the back of Mack Industries. Behind the dogs was a tall chain-link fence. Behind the fence was an empty field. No one was in sight.

"Nice doggies," she said, her voice trembling.

The dogs, all twenty of them, growled.

Out of the corner of his eye, Bobby watched Lerner, or rather, he watched her feet jiggling under her favorite carrel in the back. In the middle of the night, he had remembered that Lerner told Ripper she had a surprise named Fip. Now he was determined to find out what it was all about. He'd searched on the Internet under every possible spelling of the name. *Fhip. Fip. Fipp. Phip. Fhiph. Fiph.* All he learned was that FIP stands for Feline Infectious Peritonitis, which was some kind of virus that cats get. He was just about to give up when Lerner had arrived, looking like she was going to pop.

The bell was about to ring. He crept around the Fiction section to the very back of the library. The *XYZ* shelf ended right behind Lerner's carrel. He crept over to the Zs. Lerner's back was to him. He stood on a footstool and read her experiment over her shoulder.

Slowly, the pieces began to fit together. He didn't have all the pieces, so the picture wasn't seamless. But he figured that Lerner had some magic creature called a Fip that ate words and made things disappear. Things like Ripper. Now she was going to do something with Attackaterriers. Bobby didn't really care for Attackaterriers, but he knew right away that the Fip creature was an incredible find.

Lerner Chanse

Experiment

Fip will eat this word: Attackaterriers

Hypothesis: All Attackaterriers will disappear.

Result:

Fip will eat these words:

Hypothesis: Just   will disappear

Results: It worked!

He climbed down from the stool. He had to get that Fip.

In the hot and brilliant sunlight, Lucia Torrez broke into a sweat. Stay calm, she told herself. Maybe they'll think you're too skinny to eat. Then she remembered dogs *like* bones.

She took a step backward. The dogs took a step toward her.

"Nice doggies," she whispered, tears filling her eyes. "Please, for once, be nice doggies."

Lerner's forehead was damp with sweat. What was Bobby Nitz doing behind her? He probably didn't see anything, but it made her nervous. She watched Fip's body as he munched. Hurry. Hurry. Hurry.

Fip tried as hard as he could, but the letters were stickly in his throat. It was hard to eat with her alarm chemicals blasting.

Fip had eaten *A-t-t-a-c*. Hurry up, Lerner thought. The bell is going to ring.

The dogs began moving toward Lucia as if they were of one mind, their white teeth gleaming in the sunlight.

Without turning around, she tried turning the doorknob. Locked. Three dogs led the pack, their eyes pinned to Lucia, their tongues hanging out, their stubby tails vibrating like electric drills. *Closer. Closer. Closer. Closer. Closer.*

Lerner could feel Bobby Nitz creeping up behind her. Closer and closer. He had seen Fip! Fip was almost finished eating, but she couldn't wait. She'd have to make a run for it.

The bell rang. Lerner jumped up, knocking Bobby to the floor, and ran out the door, holding her notebook in front of her like a tray. She ran down the hall and ducked into the girls' rest room and looked at her experiment. Fip had done it! He had eaten *Attacka!*

Lerner grinned and put him in his bottle. "Good going, Fip!" she said. "Now we have to find out if it worked!"

Lucia screamed. The dogs leaped for her, giving off some kind of strange, shimmering light. She crouched and closed her eyes, expecting to feel the pounce of nails and teeth.

Instead, a wet tongue licked her cheek.

She opened her eyes. All around her, terriers were panting and wagging their tails!

Lucia didn't move. One of the dogs nuzzled her shoulder.

"Nice doggies?" she whispered.

"Yip! Yip!" barked the dogs, cheerfully.

*   *   *

With his dazzling smile, Mr. Mack was answering the questions of Ms. Ferret, the FBI official, as they finished the tour of the "Mack Technical School."

Suddenly, he stopped. A little shiver went up his spine and tingled his brain. He gasped.

"Something wrong?" asked Ms. Ferret. She was a petite, unsmiling woman wearing a wrinkled khaki suit and dark green sunglasses.

Mr. Mack blinked. What had just happened? It felt as if his brain had gone a little numb. He couldn't explain it.

Ms. Ferret continued with her questions. "How does the Attacka method work?"

"I—I don't know."

"Your advertisements say it's top secret. But this is the FBI you're talking to, Mr. Mack. Besides, it may help with the thumbtack investigation."

Archibald Mack racked his brains. He knew that he was the creator of the secret Attacka method. But what was the secret? He couldn't remember.

"Do you have something to hide, Mr. Mack?"

The investigator's voice snapped him to attention. He did have something to hide. Those children that Ms. Ferret had just seen writing "Frio Re Bampas" were his workers. If the FBI discovered that, they'd throw him in jail. He had to concentrate. He had to avoid any more questions and get rid of her.

"Well, thank you for flying to the island. I'm so glad you had the chance to see my school in session. Of course, I didn't need to start a school. But the local school is poor. And I adore children." He smiled and escorted her out. "Please call if you have any more questions, my dear."

At the word *dear,* a vein popped out on Ms. Ferret's temple. "The name is Ferret."

They walked out, and Ms. Ferret stopped short. She stared at the large holding pen for outgoing dogs that stood to the right of the main gate. Twenty cute terriers were playing and wagging their tails inside the pen.

"Isn't that odd? Those same dogs growled at me on my way in," Ms. Ferret said. "Aren't they always vicious?"

Mr. Mack stared. Those were the dogs that were ready to be shipped out. Yet, it looked as if they hadn't been trained!

If the thumbtacks and the Attackaterriers were gone, then he had nothing! Well . . . at least he still had the children to work for him, he thought. As soon as this bag of sand named Ms. Ferret was gone, he'd make the children work harder.

Ms. Ferret said good-bye and zoomed off in her rental car. After driving a mile or so, she picked up the car phone and called FBI head-quarters. "I don't have any news about thumb-tacks, but I think there's a deeper mystery here. I copied down a clue from the classroom." She held up her notebook. *"Frio Re Bampas.* Can you ask our translator to tell me what it means? I have a feeling it doesn't mean 'See Spot Run.'"

Lucia popped up from her hiding place in the backseat. "That's Bellitan. It means: Free the Children!"

Lerner waited until the hallways were quiet, then she hurried to her locker. Keeping Fip in her locker seemed less risky than carrying him around. She couldn't wait to find out if anything happened with Attackaterriers. Although late for class, she stopped at the pay phone and called Kenneth's Kennel.

"I'm interested in Attackaterriers," she said. "Do you have any for sale?"

There was a pause on the end of the line. "Well, I gotta lotta terriers. Cute dogs. Nice pets."

"You have no Attackaterriers, but you have terriers?"

"Yeah. I did have Attackaterriers. But some-how they . . . well, changed."

"How could that be?"

"I gotta admit, I'm stumped," Kenneth said.

Lerner hung up. Ha! Fip took the Attacka out of Attackaterriers!

By the time she got to class, Mr. Droan was already taking roll. Bobby Nitz ran in, breathless, just after Mr. Droan had closed his grade book.

"Ah. The guest of honor arrives," Mr. Droan said. "So glad you're joining us, Nitz."

Bobby slid into his seat.

Oh, go pick on someone your own size, Mr. Droan, Lerner said to herself, or I'll have Fip eat your grade book.

"As you people know, I gave you all detentions until the return of the photosynthesis exams," Mr. Droan began. "Well, there seems to be a development."

Reba and Randy grinned at each other.

Mr. Droan pulled a note from his desk drawer. "I found this on my desk this morning. It reads: 'Look for the tests in Nitz's locker. Signed, Anonymous.'"

"That's a lie!" Bobby shouted.

The room hushed.

"Well, if you didn't do it, then you won't mind if we search your locker."

"Be my guest."

Mr. Droan smirked. "I already did!" He heaved a stack of tests onto his desk.

Bobby was so shocked, he couldn't even protest.

"Looks like the mystery is solved," Mr. Droan said. "Bobby, you're going to the principal's office."

Lerner caught Reba smiling at Randy and realized that they had framed him. They had reproduced the tests, which was easy to do because they were sample tests from the book. Then they put them in Bobby's locker.

The joy she had felt in taking the Attacka out of Attackaterriers evaporated. She was the one who had deleted the tests, and now Bobby was getting framed for it. The right thing to do would be to speak up now. But if she told the truth, then she'd get into more trouble. And what would happen to Fip? She opened her mouth, but nothing came out.

"I'm escorting Bobby to Mrs. Norker's office," Mr. Droan said. "Nobody move a muscle until I get back."

As soon as they were gone, the class erupted.

"You put those tests in Bobby's locker, didn't you?" Lerner yelled at Reba. "That's what you were plotting yesterday after school and this morning on the bus?"

Reba grinned. "I have no idea what you're talking about. But isn't it excellent?"

"You SLUGs should be happy," Randy said. "Now we don't have after-school detention."

"She's not happy," Reba teased, "because she's in love with Nitz."

Lerner reddened. "I am not! I just don't think somebody should get in trouble for something he didn't do."

Reba stuck her chest out. "And how do you know he didn't do it?"

That shut Lerner up.

"Drop it, Reba," Sharmaine said. "The only person who is in love with anybody is you. You're in love with yourself."

"Ha. Ha. Ha," Reba said. Her glare practically set Sharmaine's hair on fire.

Lerner tried to calm down and think things through. It was all so complicated. She should never have messed with the tests or the vending machine or Ripper. Why had they all seemed like such good ideas? She needed time to think. She decided to get Fip and ditch school. She'd walk over to Ellsworth Park and spend the rest of the day alone. She grabbed her backpack and headed toward the door.

"Where are you going?" Reba asked.

"None of your business."

Winny the SLUG called after her. "But Mr. Droan said not to move a muscle!"

Lerner ran back to her locker. With a pounding heart, she opened her locker door—now she was going to add skipping classes to her list of sins—only to discover that Fip's bottle was gone. Lerner choked back a scream and pulled out every book and paper. Her experiment notebook was gone, too.

Footsteps sounded in the hallway. Was it Mr. Droan?

It was Principal Norker _____ down the hall. Mr. Droan was p_____ back to his classroom. He'd find _____ that she was gone.

Lerner and Bobby caught eyes. _____ expression crossed his face. In th____ Lerner realized that he knew why she ____ rum-maging through her locker. He knew that Fip was gone! That meant that he must have taken him! He must have done it right after she put him in, right before they both showed up late to Droan's class. He wanted Fip for himself!

"Clean up this mess and get back to class," Mrs. Norker scolded.

Lerner clenched her teeth and tried to catch Bobby's eye again, but he wouldn't look.

Mrs. Norker led Bobby down the hall. "Bobby, you'll serve your suspension in the library until your parents arrive to pick you up."

Lerner stuffed everything back in her locker, trying to figure out what to do next. How much did Bobby know about Fip? Even if he didn't know how the magic worked, he could do something horrible by accident. He could let Fip crawl around on the phone book and eat Washington, D.C., into oblivion, person by person. She had to get Fip back before anything happened.

Bobby sat in the back carrel of the library. He took the bottle out of his backpack, set it down

, and wiped his sweating palms on His chest tightened with panic. He had reature. He had the power. Now all he eeded was the guts to use it.

He pulled a memo out of his back pocket. He had taken it from Norker's office when she wasn't looking because the name on the memo— Mr. Markus Droan—had caught his eye. Markus Droan. It looked like fine worm food to Bobby. He spread the memo out on the desk. Why should he care about anybody? Everybody thought he was always to blame, so he might as well do something really horrible.

With trembling fingers, he placed the worm on the letter *M*.

To: All faculty
From: Principal Norker

Markus Droan's suitable proposal to use the Sports Equipment Fund money (which students earned over the summer by selling cupcakes) to buy a new copying machine has been approved. The new machine will be able to produce ten work sheets every second!

Fip stalled, sniffing at the ink. Something about this boy's vibration felt wrong. Where was the girl? He knew from experience that strange things happened when he ate. Now, this boy wanted to feed him. That was suspicious. Well, he wouldn't eat a smatch! Not until Lerner came back. Nobody could force him to eat.

"Do it!" the boy hissed, and poor Fip jumped. What if the boy got so angry, he squashed him? Fip sniffed the letter *M* again. Maybe it wasn't a bad idea to eat just a little.

Lerner ran down the hallway. Outside the library door, she collided with Mr. Droan.

"Ms. Chanse, why aren't you in class?"

"It's an emergency!" She plowed in ahead of him.

Bobby's untied sneakers stuck out from under her favorite carrel.

"Bobby!" she hissed.

"Go away," he whispered and hunched over the carrel.

Lerner got a glimpse of a piece of paper. "Let me see." She pushed his arm away. Fip was eating Markus Droan!

"Ms. Chanse, come back here right now!" Mr. Droan called out.

The handful of other students in the library looked up.

"Bobby, stop!" She tried pulling him out of his seat.

"You did it to Ripper," Bobby said.

Mrs. Popocheskovich started walking toward them.

Lerner ducked behind Bobby's carrel. "I was terribly wrong. I shouldn't have. Bobby, you can't delete a human being!"

"Don't stop me! I hate Droan. He makes me feel like dirt," Bobby yelled and pushed her away from his desk. She fell against a table and knocked a globe to the floor.

"Cookies, stop this . . . ," Mrs. Popocheskovich's voice trailed off.

Lerner and Bobby both looked up. Mr. Droan's body was shimmering, as if he were made of a million tiny parts and each part was beginning to head off in a different direction. His eyes shifted to the right; his mouth shifted to the left. "Onnne more word and you twooooo are out," he said in a wavering voice. Then he put his hand to his throat and said, "Doess my voiccce sound strannnge?"

No one in the library moved or spoke. The horrible sight of a living human being disappearing before his eyes sobered Bobby. He lunged for the paper. "Okay, I'll stop."

"Wait!" said Lerner, and grabbed his hand. "The only thing to do now is to let him keep eating. If we let him eat the phrase, 'Markus Droan's suitable proposal,' then the proposal will disappear, not Mr. Droan." She leaned in toward Fip and whispered, "Come on, Fip, eat some more!"

Fip moved over to the apostrophe and sucked it up.

The teacher was walking toward them, undulating with each step like a walking anemone. "Dooo yoooou waaant a detennnntion, toooooo, Ms. Chansssse?" he said.

"Markus." Mrs. Popocheskovich moved toward Mr. Droan uncertainly, extending her hand.

Fip ate the "suit" of *suitable,* then twisted up with a horrible gizzard ache.

Bobby looked at Lerner, and Lerner looked at Bobby. Fip had eaten the words: *Markus Droan's suit!* They looked at Mr. Droan. The teacher's body solidified, but his suit was shimmering.

"What the devil—" Mr. Droan looked down.

One second.

Two seconds.

Three seconds.

The hair on Mr. Droan's arm's prickled. He felt a rush of cool wind around his legs. He looked down and his eyebrows jumped up. There he was in his striped boxer shorts. His suit had disappeared!

Mr. Mack was perched at his office window when a swarm of cars approached the Mack Industries gate. Children and puppies poured out of the thumbtack factory and the Attackaterrier training facility.

Ms. Ferret got out of the leading car and put a megaphone to her mouth.

"Archibald Mack. You're under arrest for violating child labor laws. Children are not slaves. Surrender now."

Lucia hopped out of the car, jumped up on the hood, and waved a white banner.

The children cheered. The puppies yipped.

Lucia leaned over to the large Mack Industries sign and flung her banner over it. Ms. Ferret threw her a lipstick and in bright red Lucia wrote: *Re Bampas Este Frio!*

"The children are free!" she yelled.

The children and puppies went wild. "Yip! Yip! Yippee!"

Hee. Hee.

It started with a giggle from someone over in the Poetry Nook and pretty soon everybody in the library was laughing. For a few seconds, Mr. Droan stood there with his knees as white as headlights and his eyebrows going up and down like psychotic windshield wipers, then he covered up his striped rear with a newspaper and waddled out faster than anyone had ever seen him move.

The bell rang. In the chaos that followed, Lerner scooped Fip back into the bottle and ran. Bobby was right behind her. Principal Norker caught them both. Mrs. Nitz was there, wringing her thin hands.

"It's my fault," Lerner heard herself saying. "Bobby didn't do anything."

She could feel Bobby's surprised eyes on her. She was surprised herself. Bobby had stolen Fip and, even worse, had intended to delete a teacher. But she couldn't help feeling at fault. She shouldn't have brought Fip to school and she shouldn't have experimented on anything living. It was too dangerous, and the consequences were too unpredictable.

Mrs. Norker glared at both of them. "Tell me exactly what's going on here."

Lerner pushed up her glasses. If she told the truth, it would be the end of her private experiments with Fip. Keeping Fip a secret all to herself was exciting, but the responsibility was becoming overwhelming.

Lerner took a deep breath and handed Mrs. Norker the bottle. She told them about Fip and how whatever he ate disappeared. As Mrs. Norker and Mrs. Nitz listened, the wrinkles on their foreheads kept getting deeper.

Lerner imagined what would happen next: The principal would run to her office and call the FBI. The FBI's Division of Unexplained Phenomena would assign the X-Files team to confiscate and study the worm. Tearfully, Lerner would say good-bye to Fip, but she'd receive a Medal of Honor for discovering a new species and become the youngest person to be appointed X-Files Consultant. Every day after school, they'd want her to go over to the FBI building and help with Fip-related research. Maybe they'd even allow her to skip school entirely and serve the nation by working for the FBI.

Mrs. Norker held Fip's bottle up and looked at the worm inside. "If you think this is funny—"

"No!" Lerner said, "I—"

"Telling crazy fairy tales isn't going to help. I'm calling your parents, Lerner." She turned to Mrs. Nitz. "I suggest you take your son home and have a long talk with him about all this. First thing on Monday morning, we'll have a conference. I'd like your husband here, too, Mrs. Nitz, and both your parents, Lerner." She shook her head and handed Fip's bottle to Lerner. "You'd better own up to the truth."

While Mrs. Nitz and Mrs. Norker worked out the details for the meeting, Lerner stood holding the bottle in a confused fog. Lerner had spilled her guts and they didn't believe her. Now what? They weren't going to let her or Bobby off the hook without an explanation, but if they didn't believe the truth, then what could she and Bobby do?

She glanced over at Bobby. He was staring at her. Like it or not the two of them were caught in the same net.

On the ride home, Lerner's parents were mad, but they were willing to hear her side of the story. She tried to explain the whole thing about Fip to her parents. They listened quietly and then her mother said that maybe they should all see a really nice kind of doctor. Lerner knew what that meant. They thought she was crazy.

She spent the night in her room, trying to figure out what to do next.

Bookworm's Desk Calendar

Saturday
6
October

"The Todal gleeped."
—James Thurber
The Thirteen Worms

Lerner woke to the sound of Mr. Nitz shouting. She jumped out of bed and ran to the window. Bobby was sitting on his back steps, staring at his shoelaces. Lerner opened the window wider.

"You have nothing to say, do you?" Mr. Nitz was saying. "Well, that's because you don't even have half a brain."

The words hung in the air like a black cloud.

Lerner grabbed a piece of paper. If Fip could take the Attacka out of Attackaterriers, he could take the meanness out of Mr. Nitz. She wrote in tiny letters: *Mr. Robert Nitz's meanness toward Bobby*

Last night, she had promised herself no more risky experiments, but this one felt right.

Fip was hungry, and the tiny letters went down quickly.

Lerner looked out her window.

"Look at me when I'm talking to you," Mr. Nitz said.

Bobby looked up. Mr. Nitz froze and then shivered, as if an invisible creature had scurried up his spine. His neck lengthened and then his whole body relaxed. He shook his head, confused. "I don't know what got out of me. I mean, what got into me."

Bobby's chest tightened. Warily, he looked at his father, waiting for another insult to fly.

Mr. Nitz looked back at him with clear eyes. "I feel a little funny. Funny in a good way. How about you?"

"How about me?"

"Yes."

"You're asking me how I feel?" Bobby squinted up at his dad.

Mr. Nitz shrugged, smiling. "Seems like a simple enough question."

"It's just that you don't usually say stuff like that."

"I don't? Well, old dogs can learn new tricks." He sat down next to Bobby on the steps. "We were talking about Ripper, weren't we?"

The tightness in Bobby's chest moved to his throat. Why wasn't his father yelling at him? "You won't believe me. But I swear I didn't let Ripper out."

Behind the curtain in her room, Lerner winced. Bobby was going to tell his dad that it was her fault. She closed her eyes and waited to hear him blurt it out.

"Maybe it isn't anybody's fault," Bobby said. "Maybe Ripper just got out."

Lerner opened her eyes and breathed a sigh of relief. Bobby Nitz was not a tattler.

"Maybe you're right," Mr. Nitz said.

Bobby looked up, surprised that his father was agreeing. He caught sight of Lerner in her window.

She ducked behind the curtain. Inside her room, she gazed down at the magical little worm in her hand. "Go, Fip!"

Fip could sense an incredible energy vibrating from Lerner's entire being. This was more like it. All the tension of yesterday melted away, and Fip skinched around on her palm with joy.

Later on in the day, the Nitzes came over to talk about the "school situation," as Mr. Chanse said. Lerner didn't stare at Mr. Nitz, although she wanted to. She could tell he'd changed, though, in a matter of minutes. There was a bright, pleasant atmosphere in the room, even though they were gathered to talk about serious school problems. And Mrs. Nitz kept looking over at her husband with the same expression you see on people's faces when they open their doors in the spring and discover that all their daffodils have bloomed.

Mr. Chanse cleared his throat. "Well, I have to say I'm confused. It sounds like we've got a big mess here. I'm sure that one person isn't to blame for everything. I think we'll be able to sort it out if you each accept the blame for whatever mistakes you made."

Lerner nodded. She knew it was pointless to tell the truth. Parents preferred simple apologies. "I took a dare that would have gotten Bobby into trouble. And I stole candy bars and quarters from a vending machine. And I was really the one responsible for getting rid of Mr. Droan's tests. . . ." She hoped they wouldn't ask how. "And I can't really say what happened to Ripper, but I wished he would disappear." She stopped.

Bobby cleared his throat, and everybody looked at him. He was sitting on the edge of a cushioned footstool, jiggling his feet, one on top of the other. "I did a lot of wrong things," Bobby said.

There was a long, awkward silence. Lerner held her breath. He didn't sound the way he sounded when he was talking back to Mr. Droan or Ms. Findley.

"I hate it," he finally said and looked up. "I hate it."

"Hate what?" Mr. Chanse asked.

"School. The MPOOE Club. Everyone in it." His words were like the red-hot coil of an electric broiler, and the truth of his hatred radiated out like heat.

The grown-ups shifted back a little in their seats. It wasn't exactly a detailed confession, but the emotion underlying what he said was so big that they didn't want to push it any further.

"Well then," Mrs. Chanse said. Everybody stood up.

The Chanses grounded Lerner, made her apologize to Bobby, gave her extra chores to pay for the candy bars, and told her that she had to write letters of apology to Mr. Droan and to the owner of the vending machine (returning the money as well).

Mr. Nitz grounded Bobby and told him to apologize to Lerner. Then Mrs. Chanse invited them for a potluck a week from Monday. "I had no idea the Nitzes were so nice!" she said as she closed the door.

In private, both Lerner and Bobby got long lectures from their parents about how they couldn't let the MPOOEs bother them and how they had to do the right thing no matter what kind of peer pressure they were up against. Lerner and Bobby both nodded through the lectures, knowing that it wasn't as simple as their parents made it sound.

That night, just as Lerner was falling asleep, she heard a thump against her window. She looked over and saw something sticking to the glass. A paper airplane with a suction cup ingeniously attached to the tip. She raised her window and peeled it off. There was a message inside.

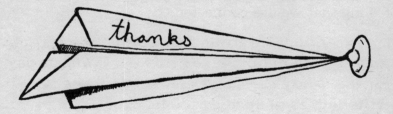

Dr. William Jay
Figer National Observatory
Astronomy Lab
Tucson, AZ 78734

Avalanche Woman
c/o Mountain View Convalescent Center
Anchorage, Alaska

Dear Ms. Avalanche:

I'm sorry I cannot address you by your name. I
don't know it. I have read about your extraordi-
nary case. I'm writing in the hopes that you can
help me. Last week, I lost the power of speech from
a shock. Perhaps you read about me in the newspaper? I feel words in my throat like prickles of
light in the dark sky, but when I open my mouth
nothing comes out.

I read that your recovery is complete and had   .
something to do with spinach soufflé? Please come
to Tucson at my expense and help me. I have this
feeling that we are connected.

Yours truly,
William Jay

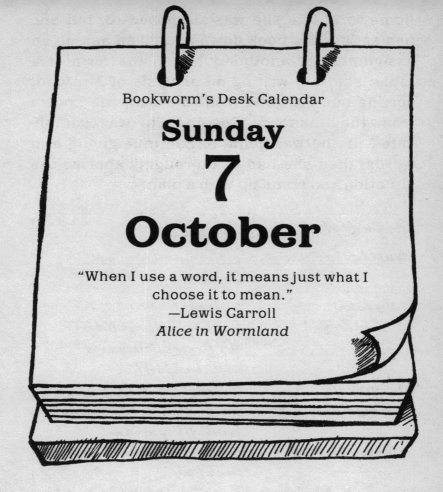

Sunday
7
October

"When I use a word, it means just what I
choose it to mean."
—Lewis Carroll
Alice in Wormland

Late morning sun streamed through Lerner's
bedroom window, spreading out on her yellow
quilt like butter on top of French toast. She was
sitting up in bed, still in her pajamas, still under
the covers, with a pad of paper resting on her
knees. She had been trying to do some science

homework, like she was supposed to, but she had set her textbook down and given herself an assignment of another kind. In the form of a table, she was writing an analysis of Fip food, sorting out the good from the bad, the known from the unknown. Feeding Fip was complicated. If she was going to continue giving him words, then she had to thoroughly analyze the situation and come up with a plan.

Analysis of Fip Food	
What I know has disappeared	The Consequences (Bad? Good? Don't know?)
1. Jay's Star	Don't know.
2. Spinach Soufflé	Don't know? Good for me. Bad for Mrs. Gormano? (Is she having a nervous breakdown?)
3. September 1	Don't know! This was really stupid.
4. Vending Machine No. 203	Bad. Fun at the time, but if the police find out will they arrest me?
5. Photosynthesis Exam	Bad. Fun at the time, but definitely trouble later.
6. Ripper, the Attackaterrier	Very bad. A mistake to delete something living.
7. Attacka	Don't know. Good, I think. But I'm not sure.
8. Markus Droan's suit	Bad, I guess. Funny but not okay.
9. Mr. Robert Nitz's meanness toward Bobby	Good.

One good, four bads, and four don't knows. Not exactly a great record. Lerner wasn't sure what to do next. She needed time to find some answers, but, unfortunately, Fip needed food. She took Fip out of his bottle and sat on her bed. The worm looked up at her hopefully. She could see his facial features quite well now. He had grown a dark, rosy brown and was about the length of a large paper clip. One week and he had quadrupled in size!

"Maybe you could learn to eat dirt for a little while," she said. "Just until I get a few things straightened out in my mind." She pinched a bit of dirt from her ivy plant onto a shoe box lid and put Fip in the middle of it. She set it on her bed and lay down next to it. "Just relax and try it," she said, and closed her eyes. "Worms like dirt." She'd relax, too, and let Fip be a regular worm for a minute or two.

Lerner's quilt was toasty and soft. She snuggled her head in the crook of her arm and fell asleep.

Fip sniffed at the dirt for a while, trying to work up an appetite. But he finally gave up and skinched off the lid to search for something tastier. He wriggled until he came to a book open at the foot of the bed. Now this was more like it. He climbed on, found an ummy word, and began to chew.

Lerner's eyelids drifted open. She lifted her head and glanced at the shoe box lid. "Fip?"

Her heart started pounding. She scanned the bedspread and saw her science book open at the bottom of the bed. Lerner grabbed the book, open to an illustration of photosynthesis. There! There was Fip inching up to the letters *e* and *n*. The beginning of the word was already gone. Lerner's brain started racing to the boom of her heart. What is it that plants give off?

Oxygen! Lerner thought. Fip is eating oxygen! *Oxy* and *g* were gone. "Fip! You can't do that! You could get us all killed." She shook Fip in her fist and began pacing.

Fip shuddered, bouncing around in the cocoon of her hand. What was wrong? Lerner's body was secreting her alarm chemical. Why was she flying around the room? Between two of her fingers, Fip saw the spinning world. The bottle on her desk was getting bigger and bigger. Fip curled into a ball, ready for impact. BAM! He hit the bottom of the bottle. SLAM! The lid crashed into place.

"You're never eating again!" Lerner yelled. She backed away and tried to calm down. Was the supply of oxygen in the air thinning? She grabbed her textbook and looked at the page.

Oxyg. Did it mean anything? She ran into the family room, where her parents were finishing their morning coffee.

"*Oxyg!* DOES IT MEAN ANYTHING? WHERE'S THE DICTIONARY?" Lerner yelled in one breath because she didn't want to waste any.

Her parents looked at each other.

Lerner grabbed the big black dictionary off her mother's desk and batted the pages until she found the *oxy*s.

> **oxycephaly**
> **oxygen**
> **oxygenate**

No *oxyg* listed. *Oxyg* wasn't a word representing a real thing, so Fip's eating had no consequences. She closed her eyes and took a big breath of beautiful oxygen. When she opened her eyes, her parents were staring at her. "Never mind," she said, and ran back upstairs.

The bottle shook as Lerner pounded into the room. Fip pressed his bristles against the glass. Lerner peered in.

"I'm sorry I was rough," Lerner said. "You're probably still hungry." A solution popped into her head. What if she fed Fip nonsense words, such as *oxyg*. She ran to her desk and got out a pen and paper. Putting down one random letter after another, she wrote: Gurkengabel. It just might work. For the first time all day, she felt absolutely giddy. She ran into the family room. Her parents shut their mouths quickly and looked guilty, as if they'd been talking about her. She smiled innocently and hoisted the dictionary to her chest. "I've got to get one of these for myself," she said, and ran back upstairs.

gurgle
gurglet
Gurkha
gurnard
guru

No Gurkengabel. Aha! No Gurkengabel. "Have a delicious Gurkengabel!" Lerner sang as she popped Fip out of his bottle. She set him on her notebook page right next to the letter *G*. "Sounds pretty good if I do say so myself. One Gurkengabel! Hold the Mustard!"

The little worm looked at the ink, then up at Lerner. She was acting strange and some of her alarm chemical lingered in the air. But he was starved. Before she could change her mind, Fip gobbled the *Gurkengabel*.

Bobby sat at the computer in his father's den, without the usual fear of being caught flapping around inside his chest like a bat in a shoe box. Through the open door, the light sound of his parents' voices drifted in. Usually his parents didn't talk at all. Most Sundays, his father worked in his office and his mother tiptoed around the house doing whatever it was that she did.

Even though he was grounded, he was having an amazing day. A lazy, ordinary, stay-at-home day. They had pancakes. And he spent the morning finishing the model bird skeleton that he had been building: wing bones—the humerus, radius, and ulna—just like his own arm bones, only light as paper. Every few minutes, he'd take a break and stick his head out the window to get a breath of fresh air. He'd look over at Lerner's window and try to imagine what she was doing.

He logged onto the Internet and sat for a few seconds, his fingers resting on the keys. What should he search for? He didn't know what she had fed Fip since yesterday. He typed in the key words: mystery and disappearance. One thousand and three matches. Too big to search. Tomorrow, he'd come right out and ask her all about Fip. But would Lerner really talk to him about it? Why should she trust him?

The thought of tomorrow weighed him down. Bobby had already decided that he wasn't going to tattle on the MPOOEs. He was hoping that would gain him a little respect. But who was he fooling? Nothing would change. Tomorrow everybody would go on hating him. Including Lerner.

Bookworm's Desk Calendar

Monday
8
October

"There is nothing . . . except the power
that you pretend to seek: the power
to grind and digest."
—T. H. White
The Once and Future Worm

A substitute sat at Mr. Droan's desk calling out
the roll. Winny Auster? Here. Randy Butler?
Here. Sharmaine Gabott? Here. Lerner Ghanse?
    The room was silent.
    "She's in the principal's office with Bobby
Nitz," Reba said.

The substitute went on.

Randy whispered to Reba, "I bet they're going to tell Norker that we put the tests in Bobby's locker."

"They can't prove anything," Reba said.

"I told you not to do it," Sharmaine said, and Reba gave her a nasty look.

After ten minutes of work sheet time, the classroom door opened and in walked Bobby, Lerner, and Mrs. Norker with the stack of blank photosynthesis exams. Lerner and Bobby slid into their seats, and Mrs. Norker addressed the class.

"We've had some behavior problems here. Lerner and Bobby have taken responsibility for their actions and have been appropriately punished."

Reba raised her hand. "What particular actions have Lerner and Bobby taken responsibility for?"

"None of your business, Reba."

The room was silent.

"If they said anything negative about the MPOOE Club, I hope—"

"Reba, I don't want to hear a word about the MPOOE Club. Enough is enough."

Mrs. Norker delivered a lecture about good behavior and told them she didn't expect to hear about any more problems. Then she passed out the exams and told them to get busy.

Reba whispered to Lerner, "You'd better not have blamed us for the tests."

Lerner smiled. "SLUGs don't need to get other people in trouble to feel powerful. Only MPOOEs do that."

Sharmaine laughed.

Lerner looked around. The principal was right. "Enough is enough." She ripped a piece of blank paper off the bottom of her exam and wrote:

> *Meeting at Recess. SLUGs ONLY. Pass it on.*

She handed it to Sharmaine who read it and passed it on. Lerner watched as the note went from desk to desk. For the rest of the period, although they worked in silence, Lerner could feel a certain bond forming among the SLUGs. She didn't know if Sharmaine was a part of it, but Lerner and the rest of the SLUGs were being connected by an invisible thread.

At recess Lerner walked over to the big oak tree, which was where the MPOOEs would often begin their powwows. After a moment, thirteen SLUGs ran over and surrounded Lerner. Bobby followed but kept quiet as the others began talking at once. The words *we* and *us* began bouncing around. What should *we* do about the MPOOEs? The MPOOEs are planning something really horrible against *us* now. The space under the tree suddenly felt like a stage with Lerner in the center under the exciting heat of spotlights.

"I have something very powerful that the MPOOEs don't have," Lerner said mysteriously.

Bobby's face fell. "You're going to tell them?"

Lerner paused.

Winny looked at Bobby and then at Lerner. "Is he part of this?"

"He knows about it."

The SLUGs digested this little tidbit of unbelievable news. Bobby Nitz, the lowest of the lowly, was in on something big.

"But is he . . . in?" Winny asked.

"He can't be in. He'll ruin everything," Julio said.

"In what?" Lerner said. "What exactly is everybody talking about?" But she knew. A thing was forming, a club, centered around her, and this was her moral moment of truth. Was Bobby in or not? Without Bobby, she had a better chance of popularity. But was it fair to exclude Bobby because of his past behavior? What if he was changing? Did he deserve a chance?

"You can't trust him," another SLUG whispered. "He's not really a SLUG."

Bobby started to walk away.

"We're not SLUGs, either!" Lerner said. "Just because the stupid MPOOEs call us SLUGs doesn't mean we are SLUGs. Bobby, wait."

Bobby turned around.

Lerner set her backpack on the ground. "I have principles. If I'm going to be part of a group then I don't want it to be a snobbish clique. Anyone can be in this group who promises to keep a secret and agrees to use the power for good, not for evil."

Everybody shut up. Bobby walked over and stood in the circle.

"I hope you know what you're doing," Bobby whispered.

Lerner did, too. She started telling them about Fip. Bobby filled in some of the missing blanks, things that Lerner didn't know about, like the thumbtack incident and how he had found articles about the disappearances of thumbtacks, spinach soufflé, and the vending machine on the Internet. The first time he talked, everybody looked at one another as if they couldn't believe they were listening to Bobby Nitz. But what he had to say was fascinating—especially to Lerner.

Everybody had a different idea about what to feed Fip next. Winny wanted to get rid of cigarettes, which she said her mother couldn't stop buying, Julio wanted to get rid of poverty, and somebody wanted to get rid of guns.

"No, all those things are too big!" Lerner said.

"How about potholes?" Winny asked.

"You guys don't get it," Lerner said. "Even something as simple as potholes can be a problem. If we get rid of potholes, then the people who get paid to fix them will be out of a job."

"Why don't we concentrate on something right here at school?" Winny said.

"MPOOEs!" Julio said.

"We absolutely can't delete people," Lerner said. "Besides, there are some people in the club who aren't so bad." She thought about Sharmaine.

"What if we deleted the MPOOE Club, not the people in it?" Winny suggested. There was a general hush.

"If we fed Fip the word MPOOEs, then the people would disappear, but if we fed him the words MPOOE Club, then the thing that holds them together would disappear. Right?" Bobby whispered.

Lerner wasn't sure. They were silent for a while. "Maybe we should try it," somebody whispered.

"We can't rush into anything," Lerner said. "Let's have another meeting tomorrow to decide."

The bell rang. Recess ended too soon. With smiles on their faces and secret knowledge in their minds, the SLUGs walked in past the MPOOEs on the basketball court.

Reba watched, biting her nails. The SLUGs were a force. How did that happen?

As soon as Lerner got home, she called up the Internet news and typed in the key word *Gurkengabel*. She expected to see "0 matches" on the screen; instead, an article appeared.

Gurkengabels Gone!

GERMANY—100,000 antique Gurkengabels (pickle forks) have disappeared from the Klunk Museum in Stuttgart. No fingerprints or clues were left. Museum officials are baffled, wondering who would want to steal Gurkengabels. Says director Frau Klunk: "The police are looking for someone with impeccable manners who enjoys the taste of a fine pickle."

Oh great! Lerner couldn't believe her rotten luck! She looked at Fip, who was asleep in his bottle. She didn't know what she could safely feed him. His little tummy rose and fell as he snored away. He looked plump enough to get by without food today. She'd have to talk it over with the others and decide what to feed him tomorrow.

Tuesday
9
October

. . . Arriety waited, trembling a little.
"Can you read?" the worm said at last.
—Mary Norton
The Borrowers

The next day at recess, Lerner, Bobby, and the other SLUGs were gathered around the oak tree. The day was crisp, the sky bright blue. The green oak leaves above them shimmered as if the sun were choosing that very moment to paint them gold.

Lerner passed around the Gurkengabel article and everyone read it with interest. "I thought I made up the word. I didn't think it was real," Lerner said. "And look what happened? This is why I'm not sure we should delete the MPOOE Club."

At that moment, Sharmaine, the MPOOE, ran over. Her face was flushed and she could hardly talk she was so out of breath. "I decided . . . I don't want to be in the MPOOE Club." She took off her MPOOE wristband and handed it to Lerner.

Lerner held it in her hand and everybody stared at it.

"She's just trying to get in so she can spy on us to the MPOOEs," Julio said.

Sharmaine looked around. "I am not."

"She thinks the MPOOE Club is more trouble than it's worth," Lerner blurted out. "Possibly the worst club on earth."

"How did you know that?" Sharmaine asked.

Lerner reddened. "I sort of read it in your journal."

"Well, you're coming over to our side just in time," Winny said. "We're about to delete the MPOOE Club!"

"We haven't agreed on that yet!" Lerner said.

Of course, Sharmaine had no idea what they were talking about. Lerner filled her in on Fip's magic. Then she turned to the group. "We don't need to delete the MPOOE Club. If Sharmaine is here, that means the club is breaking up on its own."

"You're wrong!" Sharmaine said. "I think the club is just going to get worse. Reba is going to kill me for switching sides."

Lerner could feel the pressure building. She remembered what her parents had said about resisting peer pressure, but they meant the kind of pressure that made you do bad things. If they really could get rid of the MPOOE Club that would be a good thing. Although she didn't admit this to herself, she wanted to show off a little, too. She knew how exciting it was to experience Fip's magic and knew that if she let the group in on that excitement, they would never forget it—or her.

"Okay," Lerner said. They had a few minutes before recess was over. Lerner opened her notebook and wrote:

The MPOOE Club

She set Fip down, and everybody watched in silence. Lerner wondered if they were as nervous as she was.

Fip was ecstatic. Finally some food! He realized that there were lots of eyeballs watching him, but he didn't care. He gobbled.

"Did it work?" Sharmaine whispered.

Lerner scanned the crowd on the playground.

It was hard to tell just by looking. Reba and Randy and the others were up on the basketball court. They didn't look any different.

"Check it out!" Bobby said. "Sharmaine's wristband was right there. Lerner set it down when she opened her notebook. Now it's gone."

Everybody looked at the trampled grass beneath their feet.

"They're coming!" Sharmaine whispered.

Lerner put Fip back in his bottle. Reba and Randy walked over.

"What's going on?" Randy asked, in an astonishingly innocent voice.

The SLUGs looked at Lerner.

"Are you guys starting some kind of club?" Reba asked, as if it were a completely novel idea.

"It's not really a club," Lerner said. "We were just talking about . . . about improving the school."

"Like how?" Reba asked. "And what's he doing here?" She nodded at Bobby.

"He's a part of it," Lerner said.

Reba made a face. "So what are you planning?"

"We can't trust you!" Julio blurted it out.

For five minutes, everybody argued. Some of the SLUGs didn't want former MPOOEs in the group. Lerner didn't like the idea of having Reba and Randy know about Fip. But how would they decide who to exclude and who to include? While she was thinking about that, somebody suggested coming up with a new name for the new club.

"No. No. No," Lerner said. "No club. No name. No stupid initiations to get in. Whoever wants to be on the side of good can join in."

"What is this—some kind of Robin Hood thing?" Randy asked.

"I'm in," Reba said.

"She doesn't want to be on the side of good," Winny complained. "She just wants to be in."

"I'm in, too," said Randy.

Some of the SLUGs started grumbling again. The whole thing was going to fall apart if Lerner didn't do something.

"All right. Everybody hold up your right hands," Lerner yelled. To her surprise, everyone complied.

"Repeat after me: I promise to keep this a secret."

They all chanted after her. A little tingle went through Lerner. She was pulling everybody together. No more MPOOEs. No more SLUGs. Exhilarated, she continued: "I promise not to force dares. I promise not to put people down. I promise not to get other people in trouble or boss people around." Lerner watched Reba repeat the pledge. Reba was a pain when she was queen of the MPOOEs, but now she was just another kid. Lerner would be the new leader, a wise and good leader.

More former MPOOEs noticed them and came to join. They had to do the oath again. Then, Lerner told the newcomers about Fip. She described how powerful and unpredictable the magic was—Bobby passed around the Gurkengabel article—and when it came time to decide what their next step would be, she faltered. The news about Gurkengabels was disturbing. They had to be extra careful what they fed him.

Reba interrupted in a clear, decisive voice. "Everybody here hates school, right? Let's have Fip eat *Cleveland Park Middle School.* The building will disappear, and we'll have a long vacation while they rebuild it!" She smiled and stuck out her chest, delighted with herself. The MPOOE club was gone, but Reba Silo was still a force in the universe.

Everybody started talking, clearly thrilled at the idea.

Lerner jumped in quickly. "Wait! It's too risky. What if the people in the building disappear along with the building?" she argued. "Maybe what makes a school isn't just the building but all the people in it."

Reba rolled her eyes at Lerner. "The walls and floors and roof will disappear, and all the teachers will be suddenly sitting in the dirt. It's excellent. It doesn't take a genius to figure that out."

"How do you know that people won't disappear?" Sharmaine asked. "You haven't even seen Fip eat anything."

Randy stepped forward. "Here's what we do. We delete the school during a fire drill when everybody is outside of the building."

The noise level increased, excitement was building.

"Excellent!" Reba said, beaming at him. "Randy and I will pull the fire alarm during fifth period. Once everybody's outside, Lerner will let Fip eat *Cleveland Park Middle School!*"

Students cheered.

"Let's pick something smaller," Lerner said.

"What if getting rid of the building just makes it worse?" Bobby said. "What if they send us to worse schools?"

Randy started chanting, "Erase the school! Erase the school!"

Students joined the chant.

Reba hushed the group and said, "Lerner, you're with us, aren't you?"

The way Reba wormed her way in and started taking over bugged Lerner. Reba was not the leader, couldn't everybody see that? Lerner had to get the control of the group back, but how? The excitement about deleting the school now had a life of its own. If Lerner said no, the others would think she was a spoilsport and go with Reba.

Why not go through with it? Cleveland Park Middle School was just a building, she told herself. If everybody was outside of the building, then nobody would get hurt. After it was over, she could hide Fip in her room and tell all the other kids that she couldn't find him. She'd do this one deed, which would make her popular, and then she'd retire Fip and get back to normal.

She pulled her pencil out of her pocket, pointed to the embossed label—Cleveland Park Middle School—and said, in a voice that didn't even sound like her own: "Looks like worm food to me."

Bobby looked shocked. Everybody else cheered.

The bell rang, and they had to go in.

Lerner ducked in the library. Mrs. Popocheskovich took one look at her face, brought her into her office, and closed the door.

"All right, Cookie, what's sitting on that brain of yours?"

Lerner opened and closed her mouth. All she could think about was that by the end of the day, this very library wouldn't exist. She looked out Mrs. Popocheskovich's office window into the library. Lerner loved this place the minute she first walked in. She loved the way the sun came through the big high windows and warmed up the dark wooden tables. She loved the Poetry Nook with the polka-dotted bean bag chairs and the

GREAT QUOTES bulletin board, and all the African violets on top of the high shelves. Most of all she loved the feeling that she got whenever she walked in. Her old yellow bedroom in Wisconsin used to give her the same feeling: a sense of home.

The school building wasn't the problem. Bobby was right. Deleting it would just make it worse. Why didn't Lerner just say no to Reba and the others?

Lerner looked at Mrs. Popocheskovich's patient face. "It's . . . it's . . . things are getting out of control."

Mrs. Popocheskovich nodded.

On the wall, there was a poster of an open book with a dragon flying out of its pages: WORDS ARE MAGIC. READING IS THE KEY.

"I'm glad that you came here, Lerner. I want this library to be a haven for you cookies. I worked like a cow this summer making it just right."

Lerner almost started crying. "This library is the only place in the whole school I like."

"I'm sorry to hear that. You're a smart cookie. You should so much enjoy school. Maybe it's because you're new, eh?"

"It's not just me. It's the school, too. We don't do anything real in our classes. We just do work sheets. And you know the MPOOE Club?"

Mrs. Popocheskovich made a face. "Mpooe schmpooe!"

"Well, the MPOOE Club is gone. But there's another club forming and it's getting out of control."

Mrs. Popocheskovich sighed and patted her twist. "You cookies need something constructive to do all together, eh? When I was a cookie, we worked together on making a school newspaper. The power of the press! This was so much exciting! Maybe we should start a newspaper here—"

The fire alarm went off

Lerner's stomach dropped. "Oh great!"

"Don't worry," Mrs. Popocheskovich said. "I'm sure it's what you call a drill." She ushered her out into the hallway with an innocent smile. "Go on, I'll be right out."

Tears started to well in Lerner's eyes. She wouldn't feed the school's name to Fip even if it meant losing popularity. She opened her pack—she'd make Mrs. Popocheskovich take him.

But Fip was gone! The ink bottle was nowhere in sight. Lerner rummaged through her pack.

"Outside now!" Mrs. Norker swept Lerner toward the exit.

"But somebody stole my—my—"

"We'll worry about that later."

Somebody took Fip and was going to feed him the school's name, Lerner thought. She looked back at the library. "Mrs. Popocheskovich! It isn't just a drill. Make sure you come out!"

"She will." The principal ushered Lerner into the sunlight.

Students were in lines across the playground and parking lot. The seventh and eighth graders were chattering away, unaware of anything unusual. But the sixth graders were all grinning at her. They knew the plan.

Julio ran up and whispered to her, "Can I watch?"

"I don't have Fip," Lerner said. "Somebody took him."

Bobby heard her and took off running. Lerner's heart fell. She should have known not to trust him; he probably wanted the spotlight all to himself. She ran after him, ignoring Mrs. Norker's shouts to get back in line. She tackled Bobby. "Give him back, Bobby!"

"I don't have him. I think they do." He gestured across the blacktop. Randy and Reba were huddled over something.

The embossed letters on the pencil were large, gold, and extra crispy, making them a bit difficult for Fip to swallow. He gripped the pencil with his bristles and munched, afraid that his kidnappers would harm him if he didn't. They were hunched over him, watching his every move.

"We should have found the words printed in a smaller type," Reba whispered to Randy. "This is taking too long." Fip had gotten through *CLEVE* and was just about to start *LAND*.

Mrs. Popocheskovich tiptoed down the hallway toward the library. Even though it was a drill, she should have been outside with all the others. But as she was leaving she remembered that she had left the hot plate for her coffee on high. She pictured her office, with all its papers, going up in flames. It would be too ironic for her to cause a fire by leaving the building for a fire drill.

She unlocked her office door and turned the knob on the hot plate to off. Then, because she figured the drill would only last another minute or two, she decided to sit down and write a memo to Mrs. Norker about starting up a student newspaper.

"Reba!" Lerner yelled as she ran. "Stop it. People might still be in there." The others followed.

Lerner grabbed the pencil out of Reba's hands. Fip had eaten the letters *CLEVEL*. She breathed a sigh of relief and pulled him off before he could eat more. *CLEVEL* wasn't a word. At least she didn't think it was.

"You spineless worm," Reba yelled at Lerner. "I knew you didn't have the guts to go through with it."

"You just want to be a big shot in front of everybody, Reba. You don't stop and think about the consequences. You don't understand."

"Just give me the worm, Lerner." Reba held out her hand. "Everybody wants me to be the leader."

The principal was marching down the hill toward them with an angry look. Lerner looked around at all the faces of her classmates. Here we go again, she thought, Reba will reincarnate the MPOOE Club.

Bobby spoke up. "I'm not following you, Reba."

"Neither am I," said Winny.

"I didn't want you guys anyway."

"I'm not following you either, Reba," Sharmaine said.

Reba made a face and walked away. The principal told them all to get back in line, and the bell rang twice, signaling that it was safe to return to the building.

As students headed back in, Lerner crouched down and put Fip back into his ink bottle. Her hands were shaking.

"That was close," Bobby said.

Lerner couldn't look at him. Now that it was all over, she felt bad about assuming that he was the thief. "I should have known it was Reba," she said.

Bobby shrugged. "I would have probably suspected me, too."

In the Helvetica Correctional Prison, graffiti was
not allowed. Desperate with boredom and self-
pity, Archibald Mack was breaking the rule. He
was huddled on his bed, pretending to read the
Bible, while scratching his life story into the concrete cell wall.

> Once I was something to be admired and
> feared. Now I am nothing. Well, at least I still
> have my looks.

A guard passing by noticed something odd
and stopped for a closer look. "Hey, what the
heck happened to your hair?"
Archibald Mack turned around, confused.
The guard peered in through the bars. "Man,
I've heard about guys going gray all of a sudden,
but that's ridiculous."
Mr. Mack jumped out of bed and pulled a
lock of his hair down in front of his eyes. Gray!
How could that be? His hairdresser had dyed his
hair blond just last week. Clevel brand hair dye
usually lasted three months.
The guard laughed and then noticed the wall
behind the bed. "Hey! No graffiti on the walls.
Scrub that scribble off right now!"

*   *   *

When the bus pulled up at the corner by the Nitzes' house, Lerner and Bobby got off. As usual, Bobby ran ahead without saying anything.

Lerner called out. "Do you want to come over? We could make a list of nonsense words to feed Fip." She surprised Bobby and herself with the invitation.

He stopped and put his hands in his pockets. "If you have a computer, we could check to make sure the words are really nonsense."

Lerner stopped. "I forgot. We're both grounded."

"Well, all my parents said was that I had to do my homework after school. I'd say this is homework."

The two walked into Lerner's house. The television blared from the family room. "We interrupt *Hot Days and Nights* for a live report about the Glevel mystery!"

Lerner and Bobby looked at each other. "Glevel!" They had forgotten all about the letters that Fip had eaten.

"Oh my Lord!" Mrs. Chilling exclaimed. Lerner and Bobby ran into the family room. Mrs. Chilling's hands were clamped on her head. Her hair, which was usually blond, was as gray as a dead mouse.

On the TV screen, a young reporter stood in front of Harriet's Hair Extraordinaire Beauty Salon. Gathered in a clump were four gray-haired, angry women. A reporter stood in front of them with a microphone.

"Glevel is the brand name of the most popular hair color in the country," said the reporter. "And now the hair color seems to be missing from store shelves and well . . . from heads! Tell us exactly what happened here." The reporter pointed the microphone at Harriet.

"After lunch, all these customers started showing up, demanding that I give them their money back," said the hairdresser. "They had all gotten dye jobs, and for some reason, the hair color vanished."

A gray-haired customer stuck her head toward the camera. "See?"

"I told them all that I'd redo their hair, but when I went for the Glevel, it was all gone."

Lerner and Bobby stared at Mrs. Chilling.

"Get out! Both of you!"

They ran upstairs to Lerner's room.

While Lerner and Bobby were talking, Fip sat in his bottle and watched their faces. They looked nervous about something and, frankly, it was making him snoozy. Lately, there had been too much rustle bustle. Too many eyeballs. Too many fingers. He was feeling used. He thought about how nice it would be to snuggle up with a few words and chew into a long silence.

The bottle opened and tipped. Fip rolled out into Lerner's hand. Did she want him to eat something else? He curled up into a comma and closed his eyes. Not hungry. He pretended to fall asleep so that Lerner would leave him alone, and she did. She put him in his bottle, and she and Bobby left the room.

Fip stretched and noticed that the bottle lid was off. He crawled up and out of the bottle and onto the open dictionary Lerner had left on her desk. He skinched across the page, looking down at the black morsels he was crawling over. Once he would have regarded the feast beneath his bristles with joy. But lately, people's alarm chemicals blasted the air every time he ate. He was losing his appetite. And without an appetite, he had to ponder the meaning of life itself.

He skinched over the page, pondering away, when he bumped into something. A thin white worm, no bigger than a staple, climbed over him, probing her little bristles over every part of his body.

"Hey!" Fip yelled.

"You don't feel like a bookworm," the worm said, touching his eyelids. "You can see."

Fip nodded. Then, remembering she couldn't see, said yes. She skinched down and sat in front of him.

"Me llamo Poly. Ich heiße Poly. Je m'appelle Poly. My name is Poly," said the worm.

"Oh. I'm Fip. "

She held out her bristles and Fip shook them.

"So you're not a bookworm, are you?" she asked.

"I'm supposed to be a Lumbricus," said Fip. "But I don't like dirt."

"What do you like?"

"Words."

The bookworm contracted and expanded like a jack-in-the-box. "You eat words?"

Fip squirmed. "You don't?"

The bookworm whispered. "To tell the truth, I've thought of it. Words are so wonderful to read, so nourishing to the mind. But really! It's just a fantasy. One doesn't eat words! One reads them."

"You know how to read?"

"In four languages," Poly said.

"How—if you can't see?"

"Every letter has a feel. You should know that. I read with my bristles. You can't?"

Fip shook his head. Why couldn't he remember to speak up? "No," he said loudly.

Poly contracted. "You don't have to yell," she said. "What words do you like?"

Fip shrugged. "Whatever I land on. But to tell the truth, I'm a little tired of eating."

"Have you tried glue? It has a nice chew. That's what we bookworms eat—the glue in the binding of old books. Librarians dislike us, an ironic fact of life since we bookworms are so appreciative of literature. You're the one they should dislike. We don't eat the words, after all!"

Suddenly, Fip ached all over with loneliness and bewilderment. Why couldn't he be an ordinary dirt- or glue-eating worm? Unable to help it, he put his head down and cried.

"You're homesick for your clan," Poly said gently.

Fip thought about the cold face and gritty voice of the Great Lumbra. "How can I be homesick when I never had a family?"

"Why don't you come home with me?"

Fip looked at the letters spread across the page under his bristles and sniffed. "No. I'd eat something important. I'm not a bookworm, although it sounds like a lovely thing to be."

"You need to leave. Make your own destiny. Start a new clan. That's what the hero always does," Poly said.

"What do you mean?"

"The hero in every great story leaves and makes a new destiny."

"Hero?" Fip said. He liked the sound of that word. He imagined taking a big ummy bite of it. That's when the idea hit him. "Do you know how to write, Poly?"

Lerner and Bobby came back in, breathless. They were debating the pros and cons of contacting the FBI and telling them everything.

Pros	Cons
Instant worldwide fame	Probably lose Fip
Promote scientific exploration	Probably lose Fip
Get to serve as X-Files adviser	Probably lose Fip

"Let's ask Fip what we should do," Lerner said.

"He can't talk, can he?"

"No. But maybe he could give us a sign."

Lerner walked over to her desk and picked up Fip's empty ink bottle. "Fip?" She panicked. "Fip? Where are you?"

"Ssh," Bobby whispered. "Look here."

On a piece of paper, Fip was curled up next to a smudge. It wasn't an ordinary smudge; it was a message being written by a thin white worm with dark brown bristles.

Fip's ma

"Unbelievable," Bobby whispered. "That little worm is writing!"

The worm pressed down on the paper with her bristles, finishing the *a*. She wriggled over to a stale cookie and dipped her bristles in a chocolate chip. Then she crawled back and printed the letters *g* and *i*.

"Chocolate ink!" Lerner exclaimed.

"I'd eat words if they were made out of choco-late," Bobby added.

Poly printed a *c* and skinched over to Fip.

"How does it look?" she asked. "I got a bit shaky when your friends came bounding in."

"Looks fine," Fip said. "I wonder how it'll taste?"

Poly licked one of her bristles. "Not as ummy as old glue."

Lerner and Bobby stared at the message:

Fip's magic

The words were sinking in.

"He's going to eat it, isn't he?" Bobby said.

Lerner smiled at Fip. "Fip, you're incredibly smart and brave. Why didn't I think of it?" Her smiled faded. "But, it's too dangerous. What if you eat the word *Fip* and never have a chance to get to the word *magic*?" A lump formed in her throat. "Don't do it. We can figure something else out."

Fip's skin pricked, but he smiled up at her. He had to take the chance.

Poly cleared her throat. "Pardon me if I don't stay around to watch. Couldn't see a thing anyway," she said as she skinched toward the dictionary. "Adios, Fip. Auf Wiedersehen. Au revoir. Good-bye." She crawled onto Lerner's dictionary and burrowed deep down into the binding.

Fip looked up at Lerner. She was his first friend, and in spite of everything, he loved her. He waved his bristles.

"Are you sure this is what you want?" she asked.

It was now or never. He was very hungry and very excited in a calm kind of way. He skinched over to the paper and nibbled the *F*. Ummy um um! Why hadn't Lerner thought to feed him chocolate before? Quickly, he ate his name, then stopped to take account.

Something inside his gizzard was bubbling. It wasn't a bad feeling, actually, it was a kind of tickly feeling. It didn't feel at all scary.

"Keep eating, Fip!" Lerner cried.

Fip nibbled the rest of the letters.

Lerner and Bobby stood still.

"What's happening?" Bobby whispered. "Can you tell?"

One, two, three seconds.

A shiver went through Fip's gizzard. Was this the end—or just the beginning? His muscles contracted and then relaxed. He giggled and a little burp came out.

"Fip!" Lerner whispered. "Are you all right?"

The worm wriggled.

"See if he'll eat something," Bobby suggested, and handed Lerner a piece of newspaper.

Lerner ripped a piece off and gently slid it under Fip. He wriggled off.

"He's just a regular worm, now!" Bobby said.

"I can't believe it!" Lerner looked at Fip. "You may not be magic anymore Fip, but you're a genuine, Grade-A, incredible worm."

Fip beamed.

Lerner understood. Having power was a tremendous responsibility. She wasn't surprised that he might want a break from it. "So what now?" she asked.

Fip looked toward the window, and Lerner got the message. He wanted to be outside. It made her sad to think of him disappearing into the soil. Who knew what kind of predators there were out there? But if she were a worm, that's where she'd want to be.

Wednesday
10
October

"Now that things are back to normal I can get some real work done."
—Louise Fitzworm
Harriet the Spy

It was recess, and the sixth graders gathered in a circle under the oak tree.

Lerner held Fip in her outstretched hands, so everyone could see. "We are here today to give Fip his freedom. The time of magic is over. But Fip has a new life to live, new tunnels to dig, and so do we."

Bobby lifted a large rock that was under the oak tree. Three worms, two beetles, and a hundred microscopic creatures burrowed quickly back into the mud.

"I guess he won't be alone," Sharmaine said.

"What do you think he'll do down there?" Winny asked.

Lerner remembered the reference material on worms she had checked out when she first found Fip. "He'll aerate the soil by making tunnels, allowing nutrients and water and oxygen to seep in. He'll help the soil stay rich by eating dirt and decomposed stuff and then pooping all over the place. Worms are really very important."

Fip beamed. Lerner set him down and he inched his way toward an open tunnel. "Thanks for coming into our lives in the first place, Fip," she said.

"It was pretty boring before you came," Bobby added.

"Good luck down there!"

"Eat dirt and prosper!"

Fip listened to their warm words with a new sense of purpose and confidence. He was a worm, an ordinary and *very important* worm.

Just before descending, Fip turned and gave them each a nod of his head. Then he was gone.

The students were silent.

"What now?" Sharmaine asked.

There was a loud whistle. Mrs. Popochesko-vich was waving at them from the blacktop. "Do you cookies want to put your brains together to make a newspaper?" she shouted. "Come on! There are so much exciting stories to write!"

Students Win Back Money

Lerner Chanse is delighted. Two weeks ago, she and fellow sixth graders presented the school board with a memo proving that the school was intending to use student-earned money on a copying machine. Students demanded that the money be used to buy new sports equipment for recess. The school board agreed.

Service Award Winner

Mrs. Gormano wins prize for coming up with a new school lunch menu. Yesterday's hand-tossed pizza with fresh cheese was fabulous.

**Sal's House of
Spinach
Introduces
Spinach Poufflé
New Original Recipe
Come in and eat
green today!**

Former Teacher
Now Prison Guard

Markus Droan has found employment as a prison guard. "I was meant for this job," Droan said in a recent interview. "I hope all teachers who do not enjoy teaching will get out and try something else."

In National News . . .

Starless Jay to Wed

Astronomer William Jay's speech has been restored by the Avalanche Woman. After their first meeting, he was speaking. After their second meeting, they were engaged. When asked what did the trick, the Avalanche Woman said, "Some things can't be explained."

NOTICE TO CAT OWNERS

Don't worry! Medicine for Feline Infectious Peritonitis that used to be bottled under the brand name "Fip's Magic" is no longer available. However, veterinarian Henry Chanse has developed a new medicine, called "Martha's Magic." If your cat has FIP, buy some today.

NOTICE TO PICKLE FORK OWNERS

Please consider donating American pickle forks to the Klunk Museum in Stuttgart. Their collection of German pickle forks recently disappeared.

Head-Dancing Craze

Do you know how to head dance? It's the latest dance craze, which was created by Nunzy Shadel, a dance teacher in Phoenix. Students from all over the world are flocking to her studio and paying the dancing diva big bucks to learn her secrets.